U0073637

哈福

哈福

哈福

哈福

2018新制多益 LC高分關鍵書

# 聽霸

5天完勝

突破極限，完美考高分

Listening Comprehension

# 英語聽力模擬測驗

[我的第一本多益聽力入門書]

張瑪麗 ・Steve King ◎合著

[前言]

# 大家的第一本多益聽力入門書

任何一種語言，都是先從「聽」開始，就像嬰兒也是先「聽」了不少話，才開始學會「說」。所以廣泛的聽力訓練，對記憶單字、句型理解、文法組織……等學習的確獨具淺移默化的功效。要提高聽力，應選擇自己有興趣的，並且適合自己程度或稍高於自己程度的教材著手，真正紮實的練習是避免搭配文字資料來辨讀，純粹聽內容，不看書，反覆聽直到聽懂為止，這樣才能提高辨音理解能力。

「聽」與「說」是相輔相成的，因此本書所編撰的內容，均以貼近日常生活為題材，深入淺出、輕鬆自然的情境英語，不但可以增加您學習上的樂趣，更有具體實用的好處。所以，選一本適當的教材，能夠配合自己的時間，反覆聽標準 MP3，訓練聽力的敏鋭度，甚至可以一併練習對話，很快你就會驚覺耳道暢通到地球村！

本書所錄製之精質 MP3，錄音方式為 MP3 曲目中，從曲目 2 到曲目 20，以稍慢速度唸一遍，從曲目 21 到曲目 39 以一般外藉人士説話的正常速度唸一遍，讀者可視自己的喜好及程度，選擇對話速度的快慢來進行測驗。或者，以此來檢視自己，在經過幾天的聽力訓練之後，聽力程度有沒有進步了，本來可能跟不上錄音速度，或是只聽得懂較慢速度的對話，多聽幾遍反覆練習之後，再聽一次正常速度，相信你一定會有驚人的發現。

本系列書有幾大特色，能夠讓你臻至「考試輕鬆入關，旅遊放膽出關」的絕對效果，目前分別有「聽霸！英語聽力模擬測驗」、「讀霸！英語閱讀模擬測驗」，搭配學習，聽、說、讀、寫四大基本英語能力迅速加倍進化，不啻為你學習英語的神奇護照。

聽力和閱讀是學英文二個重要的關鍵，也是最難的關卡，一定要打通這任督二脈，尤其想要參加新制多益考試的人，更要加強這二項英文能力，當然每個人也都很想知道：要如何提升自己的聽力和閱讀能力？以便提高聽力測驗分數、閱讀測驗分數。

聽力測驗和閱讀測驗，二者比重一樣，所以任何一項都不能輕忽，本系列的第一本書是，先談聽力測驗；第二本書，再來談閱讀測驗。

如何強化聽力 & 閱讀能力？想要有好的學習效果，必須要針對新制多益的出題方向來考慮策略。首先要分析出在新制多益考試要具備多少的單字、文法能力，將出題可能性較高的重要單字、文法，集中起來學習才是良策；而且自己的單字、文法能力到底達到什麼程度，了解哪個領域，是自己比較弱的地方是很重要的。

新制多益考試有 13 個主要的出題方向：一般商務、企業發展、辦公室、製造業、旅遊、外食、娛樂、保健、金融 / 預算、人事、採購、技術層面、房屋 / 公司地產。不論聽力或閱讀測驗，考題都是來自這 13 個情境。

如果你第一個目標，是訓練英文聽力，那麼就先別看文章內容，跟唸所聽內容，之後再做內容比對，聽不懂的單字，就用猜的，不能為一個聽不懂的單字停下來，因為分心，會跟不上速度，很容易錯過後面的內容。

有關聽力，最好是：聽什麼，就能知其意，那麼你的英文聽力算是很棒了。如果不行的話，那麼就多做練習，練習聽力時，先別看內容，而是先依照所聽到的速度，跟著大聲唸出來，再來對照內容文字，在此同時， 要全力注意，聽本書附贈的 MP3，留意外籍老師的發音、速度和語調。如果能夠這樣長期練習，你的聽力和口說能力，會快速大躍進。

考試的勝負往往決定於困難部份的分數，像聽力測驗中的簡短對話、簡短獨白部份，閱讀測驗的單句填空、和短文填空部份，是大家比較容易掌握的部份。若想脫穎而出拿高分，一次拿到金色證書，就要在別人不會的方面下功夫。但是話又說回來，二者相較，還是基本功比較重要，畢竟得分容易，基本分數先拿到再說，接下來再進攻比較艱深的考題，才不會兩頭落空，畢竟「手上一隻鳥，勝過林中二隻鳥」。

本書是想參加多益測驗者的第一本聽力入門書，前面說過聽力測驗的簡短對話、簡短獨白部份，是大家比較容易掌握、比較容易得分的部份，所以本書先著重在這個部份，以好拿分數者為優先學習，因為，有了基礎功，比較容易穩定軍心、建立自信心，讓你在上考場前，擁有比別人有更紮實的基礎和拿分的技巧，精讀本書後，進考場前，你已經先馳得點了。

作者　謹識

## <本書特色>

★英語聽力，全勝關鍵

★提升你的聽力指數

★保持你的口語恆溫

★英語聽力，急速攀升

★加強英語聽覺敏銳度

★強化英聽考試戰備力

★英語聽力，速增 100 分

## 內容重點

★不論是用來當作模擬測驗的補充，或是平日厚實聽力的能量，都能夠讓你累積最佳戰備力與競爭力。

★迅速提升聽、說靈敏度，輕輕鬆鬆訓練聽力，也加強英語口說互動技巧，瞬間直達腦力記憶庫。

★句型簡單易說，話題新鮮有趣，完全生活情境式對話，摒除傳統枯燥乏味的內容，學習起來絕對輕鬆不打盹。

★由美籍專業播音員精心錄製的兩種標準速度，腔調純正道地，情感豐富自然，臨場感超體驗，悅聽度 100%。

# CONTENTS

第一部分

# 1 聽力測驗問題

**01. What will Mary do?**

(A) Leave the country

(B) Retake the class

(C) Retake the final exam

(D) Drop the class

MP3-02（稍慢速度）
MP3-21（正常速度）

**02. How many bottles will John drink in a month?**

(A) 4

(B) 12

(C) 6

(D) 8

MP3-02（稍慢速度）
MP3-21（正常速度）

**03. Where are Mary and Greg?**

(A) Already at the play

(B) Driving to the play

(C) Still at Greg's apartment

(D) Still at Mary's apartment

MP3-02（稍慢速度）
MP3-21（正常速度）

**04. What did Joe and Bob do?**

(A) Murder someone

(B) Bring a knife to the airport

(C) Steal purses from old ladies

(D) Hijack a tourist bus

MP3-02（稍慢速度）
MP3-21（正常速度）

**05. Why is Mr. Lin angry with his secretary?**

(A) She forgot to deliver him a message from Mr. Peters.

(B) She brought him a ham sandwich instead of a turkey sandwich.

(C) She made a grammatical error in the memorandum.

(D) She told his wife that he wasn't there when he was.

MP3-02（稍慢速度）
MP3-21（正常速度）

**06. What's Mary looking for?**

(A) Her dog

(B) Her bracelet

(C) Her watch

(D) Her necklace

MP3-03（稍慢速度）
MP3-22（正常速度）

**07. Where is John going this summer?**

(A) Hong Kong

(B) Amsterdam

(C) New York

(D) Paris

MP3-03（稍慢速度）
MP3-22（正常速度）

**08. How will Mary pay the bill?**

(A) She will get another job.

(B) She will get a loan from the bank.

(C) She's going to borrow the money from John.

(D) She will sell her car.

MP3-03（稍慢速度）
MP3-22（正常速度）

**09. What happened to John?**

(A) A dog chased him down the block.

(B) He got ran over by a car.

(C) He fell in love.

(D) He ran over a dog in his car.

MP3-03（稍慢速度）
MP3-22（正常速度）

**10. When will Mary call John?**

(A) Tonight

(B) Tomorrow

(C) Next week

(D) Tuesday

MP3-03（稍慢速度）
MP3-22（正常速度）

**11. What present did Mary get for her birthday?**

(A) A bicycle

(B) A pony

(C) A Toyota Camry

(D) A Revlon make-up kit

MP3-04（稍慢速度）
MP3-23（正常速度）

**12. What was John doing on the Internet?**

(A) He was studying for school.

(B) He was making web pages.

(C) He was looking for a job.

(D) He was surfing for the car pages.

MP3-04（稍慢速度）
MP3-23（正常速度）

**13. What does Mary usually do with her computer?**

(A) Play games

(B) Chat about boys

(C) Study

(D) Surf

MP3-04（稍慢速度）
MP3-23（正常速度）

**14. What does the teacher ask John?**

(A) Who killed Julius Caesar?

(B) Who killed Marc Antony?

(C) Who killed Pompeii?

(D) Who led the revolt of the slaves in ancient Rome?

MP3-04（稍慢速度）
MP3-23（正常速度）

**15. What is the team cheering about?**

(A) The team made it to the national championships.

(B) The team just tied with the Real Madrid.

(C) The team just beat the French national team in the World Cup.

(D) The team just won the coin toss.

MP3-04（稍慢速度）
MP3-23（正常速度）

**16. When are they going to watch the game?**

(A) Four o'clock

(B) Monday night

(C) Tonight at six

(D) Sunday afternoon

MP3-05（稍慢速度）
MP3-24（正常速度）

**17. When are they going to meet?**

(A) Sunday afternoon

(B) Saturday morning

(C) Sunday morning

(D) Saturday afternoon

MP3-05（稍慢速度）
MP3-24（正常速度）

**18. What kind of movie did they see?**

(A) Comedy

(B) Sci-fi

(C) Horror

(D) Drama

MP3-05（稍慢速度）
MP3-24（正常速度）

19. What kind of movie does Mary like?

(A) Romantic Comedy

(B) Sci-fi

(C) Thriller

(D) Drama

MP3-05（稍慢速度）
MP3-24（正常速度）

20. What are they talking about?

(A) A motocross competition

(B) A band contest

(C) A chess match

(D) The football game last night

MP3-05（稍慢速度）
MP3-24（正常速度）

**21. What does Mary come to the airport for?**

(A) To tell John goodbye

(B) To stop John from going

(C) To tell John she loves him

(D) To go with John to Florida

MP3-06（稍慢速度）
MP3-25（正常速度）

**22. How many flowers did Mary plant totally?**

(A) 9

(B) 21

(C) 8

(D) 25

MP3-06（稍慢速度）
MP3-25（正常速度）

**23. How many monkeys did John see in the zoo?**

(A) As many as sixty monkeys

(B) No more than sixty monkeys

(C) Possibly more than sixty monkeys

(D) Exactly sixty monkeys

MP3-06（稍慢速度）
MP3-25（正常速度）

**24. Why does John seem unhappy?**

(A) The neighbor ran over his cat

(B) Mary left him

(C) The neighbor ran over his dog

(D) His best friend died

MP3-06（稍慢速度）
MP3-25（正常速度）

**25. What is Mary excited about?**

(A) She aced the final exam.

(B) Paul likes her.

(C) She won a new car.

(D) She won a trip to the Bahamas.

MP3-06（稍慢速度）
MP3-25（正常速度）

**26. How often does the bus run?**

(A) Every thirty minutes

(B) Every forty-five minutes

(C) Every hour

(D) Every hour and a half

MP3-07（稍慢速度）
MP3-26（正常速度）

**27. Why does Mary need a computer?**

(A) For school

(B) To use the internet

(C) To write a book

(D) To find the first five thousand digits to pi

MP3-07（稍慢速度）
MP3-26（正常速度）

**28. What's the problem with Mary's car?**

(A) The alternator is out.

(B) The radiator is blown.

(C) The alignment is off.

(D) The gasket is leaking.

MP3-07（稍慢速度）
MP3-26（正常速度）

**29. What is John expecting?**

(A) A surprise party

(B) A kiss

(C) A necklace

(D) Money

MP3-07（稍慢速度）
MP3-26（正常速度）

**30. Why did Mary stay up last night?**

(A) She was doing homework.

(B) She was talking to John on the phone.

(C) She was watching television.

(D) She was working.

MP3-07（稍慢速度）
MP3-26（正常速度）

**31. What is John doing?**

(A) Hunting

(B) Fishing

(C) Playing video games

(D) Playing basketball

MP3-08（稍慢速度）
MP3-27（正常速度）

**32. What will Mary bring back?**

(A) Eggs

(B) Milk

(C) Green onions

(D) Ham

MP3-08（稍慢速度）
MP3-27（正常速度）

**33. Where does the conversation take place?**

(A) At an airport

(B) At the museum

(C) At a bus stop

(D) At a train station

MP3-08（稍慢速度）
MP3-27（正常速度）

**34. When will PC Life magazine stop monthly publication?**

(A) January

(B) February

(C) March

(D) December

MP3-08（稍慢速度）
MP3-27（正常速度）

**35. What is Food Lion?**

(A) A movie

(B) A book

(C) A ship

(D) A grocery store

MP3-08（稍慢速度）
MP3-27（正常速度）

**36. At what temperature will the can explode?**

(A) 100 degrees

(B) 120 degrees

(C) 130 degrees

(D) 150 degrees

MP3-09（稍慢速度）
MP3-28（正常速度）

**37. What is Mary Queen?**

(A) A dog

(B) A cat

(C) A church

(D) A ship

MP3-09（稍慢速度）
MP3-28（正常速度）

**38. Where does Mary Queen sail from?**

(A) Miami, FL

(B) New Orleans, LA

(C) Corpus Christi, TX

(D) Galveston, TX

MP3-09（稍慢速度）
MP3-28（正常速度）

**39. How long did they take to get to New York?**

(A) A month

(B) Two weeks

(C) One week

(D) Three days

MP3-09（稍慢速度）
MP3-28（正常速度）

**40. How did they get to London?**

(A) By airplane

(B) By car

(C) By train

(D) By ship

MP3-09（稍慢速度）
MP3-28（正常速度）

**41. When is the movie due back?**

(A) Monday

(B) Tuesday

(C) Wednesday

(D) Friday

MP3-10（稍慢速度）
MP3-29（正常速度）

**42. What's that advertising?**

(A) Pepsi

(B) Coca-cola

(C) Fruit of the Loom

(D) Levi's

MP3-10（稍慢速度）
MP3-29（正常速度）

**43. How was traffic that morning?**

(A) Pleasant

(B) Fine

(C) Very bad

(D) Pretty smooth

MP3-10（稍慢速度）
MP3-29（正常速度）

**44. What will they probably do next?**

(A) Shoot pool

(B) Play cards

(C) Watch television

(D) Play basketball

MP3-10（稍慢速度）
MP3-29（正常速度）

**45. Who designed the website?**

(A) Veritas Web Publishing

(B) John

(C) Luke

(D) Mark

MP3-10（稍慢速度）
MP3-29（正常速度）

**46. Who's in charge of the project, Mary or John?**

(A) Mary

(B) John

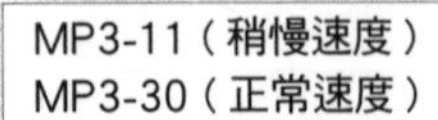

**47. Whose surprise party are they planning for?**

(A) John

(B) Mary

(C) Fred

(D) Jack

MP3-11（稍慢速度）
MP3-30（正常速度）

**48. Why was John late?**

(A) The play he and Mary went to watch started late.

(B) It took forever for the waiter to bring them their food at the restaurant.

(C) John and Mary got in a car wreck.

(D) John and Mary got in a fight.

MP3-11（稍慢速度）
MP3-30（正常速度）

**49. Where did John hunt deer?**

(A) Broken Bow State Park

(B) Beaver's Bend State Park

(C) Broken Arrow State Park

(D) Robber's Cave State Park

MP3-11（稍慢速度）
MP3-30（正常速度）

**50. Where is Mary going after she graduates?**

(A) Go back to university

(B) Europe

(C) Work at a marketing firm

(D) New York

MP3-11（稍慢速度）
MP3-30（正常速度）

**51. What should people do if they want to sail?**

(A) Rent a sailboat

(B) Steal a sailboat

(C) Go fishing

(D) Borrow a sailboat from someone at the dock

MP3-12（稍慢速度）
MP3-31（正常速度）

**52. What's wrong with Mary?**

(A) She failed her test.

(B) She broke up with her boyfriend.

(C) She's sick.

(D) She lost all of her money gambling.

MP3-12（稍慢速度）
MP3-31（正常速度）

**53. What's wrong with John?**

(A) He's sick.

(B) He lost his job.

(C) He lost his money gambling.

(D) He got lost on the freeway.

MP3-12（稍慢速度）
MP3-31（正常速度）

**54. What is Mrs. Lin worried about?**

(A) A train wreck

(B) A plane crash

(C) Getting killed

(D) Gypsies

MP3-12（稍慢速度）
MP3-31（正常速度）

**55. Where is the recorded message most likely to be heard?**

(A) On an answering machine

(B) On the television

(C) On the radio

(D) On John's voicemail

MP3-12（稍慢速度）
MP3-31（正常速度）

**56. Where does the conversation possibly take place?**

(A) On a train car

(B) At a restaurant

(C) At someone's house

(D) At work

MP3-13（稍慢速度）
MP3-32（正常速度）

**57. When does the show come on?**

(A) In one hour

(B) In two hours

(C) In three hours

(D) In four hours

MP3-13（稍慢速度）
MP3-32（正常速度）

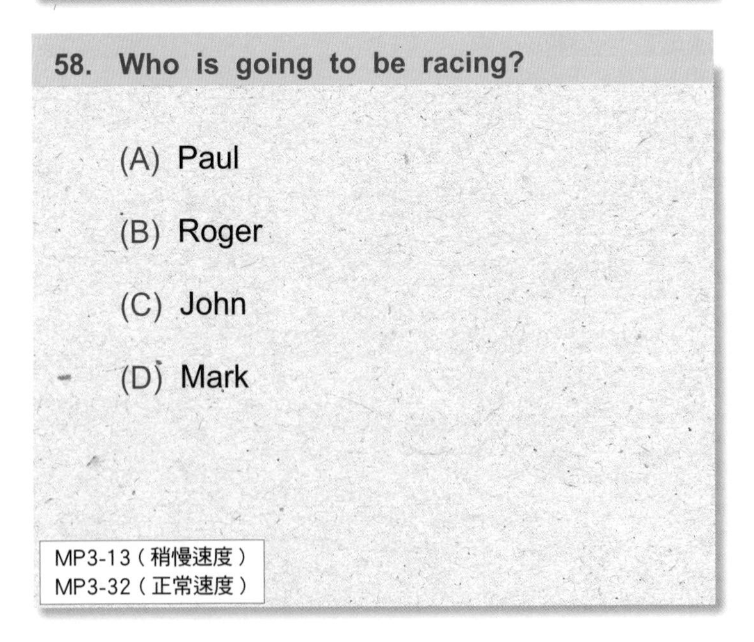

**58. Who is going to be racing?**

(A) Paul

(B) Roger

(C) John

(D) Mark

MP3-13（稍慢速度）
MP3-32（正常速度）

**59. Who won the race?**

(A) John

(B) Paul

(C) Roger

(D) Mark

MP3-13（稍慢速度）
MP3-32（正常速度）

**60. How many days has it been raining?**

(A) 1 day

(B) 2 days

(C) 3 days

(D) 4 days

MP3-13（稍慢速度）
MP3-32（正常速度）

**61. Does Man like snow?**

(A) He hates it.

(B) She's ambivalent toward it.

(C) He likes it.

(D) He loves it.

MP3-14（稍慢速度）
MP3-33（正常速度）

**62. What are they going to do?**

(A) Go to the Bahamas

(B) Go skiing in Vancouver

(C) Go skiing in Colorado

(D) Go to California

MP3-14（稍慢速度）
MP3-33（正常速度）

**63. Where does John recommend them to go?**

(A) Tokyo House

(B) Kim Long Chinese & Vietnamese Buffet

(C) Jack's Steakhouse

(D) Macaroni Grill

MP3-14（稍慢速度）
MP3-33（正常速度）

**64. Where did John go last week?**

(A) San Diego, CA

(B) Las Vegas, NV

(C) Dallas, TX

(D) Tulsa, OK

MP3-14（稍慢速度）
MP3-33（正常速度）

**65. Did Mary enjoy her trip?**

(A) Yes

(B) No

MP3-14（稍慢速度）
MP3-33（正常速度）

**66. What did Mary bring back from her trip?**

(A) Leis

(B) Pictures

(C) A coconut bra

(D) A staff

MP3-15（稍慢速度）
MP3-34（正常速度）

**67. Why would Mary give John a present?**

(A) To apologize

(B) Because it was her birthday

(C) Just because she was in a good mood

(D) For Christmas

MP3-15（稍慢速度）
MP3-34（正常速度）

**68. What did Helen do for Mary while Mary was on vacation?**

(A) Pick up the mail

(B) Get her homework for her

(C) Take messages for her

(D) Water her plants

MP3-15（稍慢速度）
MP3-34（正常速度）

**69. Was John able to pick up Mary at the airport?**

(A) Yes

(B) No

MP3-15（稍慢速度）
MP3-34（正常速度）

**70. Why didn't John call Mary?**

(A) He forgot.

(B) He was in a meeting.

(C) He was playing a game with her.

(D) His phone broke.

MP3-15（稍慢速度）
MP3-34（正常速度）

**71. How is the weather?**

(A) Sunny

(B) Rainy

(C) Snowy

(D) Cold

MP3-16（稍慢速度）
MP3-35（正常速度）

**72. Which car does John like better?**

(A) Mazda RSX

(B) Dodge Viper

(C) Jaguar XJ

(D) BMW M5

MP3-16（稍慢速度）
MP3-35（正常速度）

**73. Why is John going to the gas station?**

(A) To get some gas

(B) To get some beer

(C) To get the new issue of *Playboy*

(D) To get some cigarettes

MP3-16（稍慢速度）
MP3-35（正常速度）

**74. Did Mary bring an umbrella with her?**

(A) Yes

(B) No

MP3-16（稍慢速度）
MP3-35（正常速度）

**75. What position is John applying for?**

(A) Restaurant manager

(B) Restaurant server

(C) Waitress

(D) Window washer

MP3-16（稍慢速度）
MP3-35（正常速度）

**76. When does the bank open?**

(A) 9:00

(B) 10:00

(C) 11:00

(D) 12:00

MP3-17（稍慢速度）
MP3-36（正常速度）

**77. Did the meeting go well?**

(A) Yes

(B) No

MP3-17（稍慢速度）
MP3-36（正常速度）

**78. How much did John pay for his new car?**

(A) $5,000

(B) $10,000

(C) $15,000

(D) $20,000

MP3-17（稍慢速度）
MP3-36（正常速度）

**79. What is Mary eating?**

(A) Rice

(B) Beef

(C) Chicken

(D) Peas

MP3-17（稍慢速度）
MP3-36（正常速度）

**80. Why is John running?**

(A) For fun

(B) He's practicing for a marathon

(C) To impress a girl

(D) To lose weight

MP3-17（稍慢速度）
MP3-36（正常速度）

**81. How much is John's used car worth?**

(A) $5,000

(B) $10,000

(C) $15,000

(D) $20,000

MP3-18（稍慢速度）
MP3-37（正常速度）

**82. Who's at the door?**

(A) Fred

(B) Allen

(C) Lisa

(D) Carol

MP3-18（稍慢速度）
MP3-37（正常速度）

**83. Which book was the man looking for?**

(A) To Kill a Mockingbird

(B) Grapes of Wrath

(C) War and Peace

(D) The Rats of Nimh

MP3-18（稍慢速度）
MP3-37（正常速度）

**84. Does the bookstore carry the book the man is looking for?**

(A) Yes

(B) No

MP3-18（稍慢速度）
MP3-37（正常速度）

**85. With whom is Mary talking on the phone?**

(A) John

(B) Caroline

(C) Jack

(D) Bob

MP3-18（稍慢速度）
MP3-37（正常速度）

**86. What did the women first say when he got home?**

(A) Hey Mary, where are you?

(B) Hey, how are you doing?

(C) I'm back!

(D) I'm home!

MP3-19（稍慢速度）
MP3-38（正常速度）

**87. Where is the women's favorite place?**

(A) The park

(B) His parents' house

(C) The lake

(D) Cici's Pizza

MP3-19（稍慢速度）
MP3-38（正常速度）

**88. Where are they going for dinner?**

(A) Mack's Diner

(B) Covino's Pizza

(C) Pizza Hut

(D) Frank's Burgers

MP3-19（稍慢速度）
MP3-38（正常速度）

**89. What event is it?**

(A) The opening night of a theater production.

(B) The opening of a new building at the university.

(C) The opening night of a new movie.

(D) The Cowboys — Texans game.

MP3-19（稍慢速度）
MP3-38（正常速度）

**90. What are the two women talking about?**

(A) Mary's new puppy

(B) Mary's and John's fight

(C) The opening of the new building at the university.

(D) The new restaurant on the corner.

MP3-20（稍慢速度）
MP3-39（正常速度）

**91. What kind of school team is John in?**

(A) Math

(B) Football

(C) Soccer

(D) Chess

MP3-20（稍慢速度）
MP3-39（正常速度）

**92. What did John get?**

(A) A new puppy

(B) A new set of golf clubs

(C) A new car

(D) A new cat

MP3-20（稍慢速度）
MP3-39（正常速度）

**93. Did Mary get the piano for her birthday present?**

(A) Yes, she got the piano for her birthday.

(B) No, she got the piano for Christmas.

(C) No, she bought the piano herself.

(D) No, she got the piano for Easter.

MP3-20（稍慢速度）
MP3-39（正常速度）

**94. How's the weather where John's at?**

(A) Sunny

(B) Hurricanes

(C) A light rain

(D) Hot and dry

MP3-20（稍慢速度）
MP3-39（正常速度）

**95. What happened to the printer?**

(A) It was stolen.

(B) It disappeared.

(C) Johnny took it home with him.

(D) The paper keeps jamming.

MP3-20（稍慢速度）
MP3-39（正常速度）

▶To sensible men, every day is a day of reckoning.

----J.W.Gardnerr

（對聰明人來說，每一天的時間都是要精打細算的。）

----J・W・ 加德納

第二部分

# 2 聽力測驗解答

MP3-02（稍慢速度）
MP3-21（正常速度）

**A:** Did you hear about Mary?

（你有聽說瑪莉的事嗎？）

**B:** No. What about her?

（沒有，她怎麼啦？）

**A:** She flunked out of her class.

（她考不及格。）

Her dad is pissed.
（他父親很生氣。）

**B:** And?

（然後呢？）

**A:** Well, she has to either retake the class or drop school.

（嗯，她必須要重修否則就得退學。）

**B:** What will Mary do?

（那瑪莉會怎麼做呢？）

**A:** Well, I guess she'll retake the class.

（嗯，我猜她會重修。）

She's almost done with school, and if she just drops out, then the last three years were a total waste.

（她該修的課業差不多都修完了，如果退學，那她過去這三年全都浪費掉了。）

**What will Mary do?**

**（瑪莉會怎麼做呢？）**

(A) Leave the country.

(B) Retake the class.

(C) Retake the final exam.

(D) Drop the class.

***Answer: (B)***

## Dialogue

MP3-02（稍慢速度）
MP3-21（正常速度）

**A:** How are you doing today, John?

（約翰，你今天好嗎？）

**B:** Pretty well.

（很不錯。）

Do you still carry that wine I love so much I forgot what it was called.
（你還有賣我喜歡的那種酒嗎？…我忘記是什麼酒了。）

You suggested it to me last time I was here.
（上次我在這裡時你建議我的。）

**A:** You mean the Opus One?

（你是指 Opus One 嗎？）

We sure do.
（我們當然有賣啊。）

How many bottles will you drink in a month?
（你一個月要喝幾瓶啊？）

**B:** Oh, probably at least six. Why?

（嗯，至少要六瓶吧，為什麼這樣問？）

**A:** Well, you could buy a case of twelve bottles.

（嗯，你可以買一箱十二瓶裝的那種。）

You'll get a discount, and it will last you for two months.

（那種有折扣，而且你可以喝兩個月。）

**How many bottles will John drink in a month?**

**（每個月約翰要喝幾瓶？）**

(A) 4

(B) 12

(C) 6

(D) 8

***Answer: (C)***

MP3-02（稍慢速度）
MP3-21（正常速度）

**A:** I just got off the phone with Mary.

（我剛剛跟瑪莉通了電話。）

**B:** We've been waiting almost twenty minutes for them and the play's about to start.

（我們等他們已經快二十分鐘了。比賽都快開始了。）

Where are they?

（他們到底在哪裡啊？）

**A:** Apparently they're still at Greg's apartment.

（很顯然的，他們還在葛利格家裡。）

His car won't start and he's been trying to figure out what's wrong with it.

（他的車子發不動，一直在找問題出在哪裡。）

**B:** So they're not coming?

（那他們不來了嗎？）

**A:** Well, Mary's making him quit and call a cab.

（這個嘛，瑪莉叫他不要再試了，去叫輛計程車。）

She thinks they'll be here in twenty more minutes.

（她認為再二十多分鐘他們就會到了。）

**Where are Mary and Greg?**

（瑪莉跟葛利格現在在哪裡？）

(A) Already at the play.

(B) Driving to the play.

(C) Still at Greg's apartment.

(D) Still at Mary's apartment.

***Answer: (C)***

# Dialogue

MP3-02（稍慢速度）
MP3-21（正常速度）

**A:** Who was that on the phone?

（電話裡的是誰？）

**B:** Oh, that was Bob.

（歐，那是鮑伯。）

**A:** What did he want?

（他要做什麼？）

**B:** To tell me to get them a lawyer.

（叫我幫他們找個律師。）

Evidently, he and Joe are in jail.
（顯然他和喬在監獄裡。）

**A:** What did they do?

（他們怎麼了？）

**B:** Well, Joe had brought along his knife for the hunting trip and forgot to check it in luggage at the airport; instead he put it in his carry-on bag.

（嗯，喬帶著刀去狩獵之旅，到機場忘了放在托運的行李，而放在隨身包包裡。）

He apparently got into a heated debate with the security guards at the airport and they tossed him and Bob into jail for bringing the knife.
（結果在機場和安檢人員起了激辯，然後就因為攜帶刀子被扭送監獄了。）

**What did Joe and Bob do?**
（喬和鮑伯做了什麼？）

(A) Murder someone.

(B) Bring a knife to the airport.

(C) Steal purses from old ladies.

(D) Hijack a tourist bus.

***Answer: (B)***

# 5 Dialogue

MP3-02（稍慢速度）
MP3-21（正常速度）

**A:** I can't believe you didn't deliver me my message from Mr. Peters!

（我不敢相信你沒有把彼德斯先生的口信告訴我！）

**B:** You don't need to be so angry, Mr. Lin.

（林先生，你不用這麼生氣吧。）

**A:** But it was an urgent message.

（但這是非常緊急的口信。）

He told you it was urgent.
（他跟你說了啊。）

Why didn't you tell me about his message immediately?
（你為什麼沒有立刻告訴我呢？）

**B:** I forgot.

（我忘記了。）

I'm sorry.
（我很抱歉。）

It just slipped my mind.
（就不小心忘掉了。）

**A:** Because of you, the firm lost the Peters Account!

（就因為你，公司沒有爭取到彼得斯的業務！）

**Why is Mr. Lin angry with his secretary?**
（林先生為什麼很生他秘書的氣？）

(A) She forgot to deliver him a message from Mr. Peters.

(B) She brought him a ham sandwich instead of a turkey sandwich.

(C) She made a grammatical error in the memorandum.

(D) She told his wife that he wasn't there when he was.

***Answer: (A)***

## Dialogue

MP3-03（稍慢速度）
MP3-22（正常速度）

**A:** I lost my necklace while I was swimming over there.

（我在你那邊游泳時，把項鍊弄丟了。）

Do you mind if I come over and look for it?
（可不可以讓我過來看一下呢？）

**B:** Sure, but I haven't found anything here, Mary.

（當然可以，但是我並沒有發現任何東西，瑪莉。）

I just did a pretty thorough cleaning.
（我剛剛才好好打掃過。）

Have you checked all throughout your house?
（你有沒有好好找過你家裡呢？）

**A:** Yes, I have.

（我已經找過了。）

And I noticed it was gone right after I got home from your place.
（我發現就是我從你那邊離開回家時不見的。）

**B:** Maybe you lost it before you got here?

（也許你來之前就掉了？）

**A:** No, because I remember playing with it while I was waiting for you to answer your door.

（不可能，因為我記得在等你開門時，我還在把玩它呢。）

Can I just come over and check?
（我可不可以過來看看呢？）

**B:** I guess, but I still don't think you'll be able to find it here.

（可以，我還是覺得你不可能在這裡找到的。）

**What's Mary looking for?**
（瑪莉在找什麼？）

(A) Her dog

(B) Her bracelet

(C) Her watch

(D) Her necklace

***Answer: (D)***

MP3-03（稍慢速度）
MP3-22（正常速度）

**A:** Have you ever been to Amsterdam?

（你有去過阿姆斯特丹嗎？）

**B:** No, John. Why?

（約翰，沒有，怎麼了？）

**A:** Well, I'm going to go there for vacation this summer.

（嗯，我這個夏天要去那裡度個假。）

And I was hoping you could give me some input.
（我希望你能給點建議之類的。）

**B:** Well, I've heard it's pretty cool.

（嗯，我聽說那裡很冷。）

**A:** Yeah, me too, that's why I'm going.

（我也聽說了，所以我才會要去。）

**Where is John going this summer?**
（約翰夏天要去哪裡？）

(A) Hong Kong

(B) Amsterdam

(C) New York

(D) Paris

***Answer: (B)***

▶Reading make a full man, conference a ready man, and writing an exact man.

---Bacon

（閱讀使人充實，交談使人機智，寫作使人精確。）

---- 培根

# Dialogue

MP3-03（稍慢速度）
MP3-22（正常速度）

**A:** What's the matter, Mary?

（瑪莉，怎麼了？）

**B:** I lost my job.

（我被炒魷魚了。）

**A:** I'm sorry.

（真遺憾。）

**B:** And my rent check is almost due.

（我的房租又快到期了）

How am I going to pay the bill?
（我要怎麼付房租呢？）

**A:** You could sell your car.

（你應該把車賣掉。）

I mean, you live right next to the train station, so it's not like you need it.
（我是說，你就住在火車站附近，所以不太需要車子。）

And the money you make from it will hold you over for a while until you can get another job.
（你賣車的錢可以撐一陣子，直到你找到下個工作。）

**B:** That's not a bad idea.
（聽起來還不錯。）

**How will Mary pay the bill?**
（瑪莉要怎麼付房租呢？）

(A) She will get another job.

(B) She will get a loan from the bank.

(C) She's going to borrow the money from John.

(D) She will sell her car.

***Answer: (D)***

MP3-03（稍慢速度）
MP3-22（正常速度）

**A:** What happened to you?

（你怎麼了？）

**B:** A dog just chased me all the way down the block.

（有隻狗在街上一直追著我跑。）

**A:** A dog, John?

（約翰，你說一隻狗？）

**B:** Yeah. This thing was huge.

（嗯，那隻狗很大。）

**A:** That dog, that's outside on our front porch?

（你是說我們前門廊外那隻嗎？）

**B:** Yeah, that's the one.

（對，就是那隻狗。）

**A:** That Chihuahua the size of a football?

（就是那隻像足球一樣大的吉娃娃？）

**B:** Yeah, well, it looked huge when it was charging at me.

（對啊，嗯，不過它對我吠叫的時候看起來很大。）

**What happened to John?**
（約翰怎麼了？）

(A) A dog chased him down the block.

(B) He got ran over by a car.

(C) He fell in love.

(D) He ran over a dog in his car.

***Answer: (A)***

# Dialogue

MP3-03（稍慢速度）
MP3-22（正常速度）

**A:** Well, John called me again.

（約翰又打電話給我了。）

**B:** Are you going to call him back, Mary?

（瑪莉，你要給他回電嗎？）

**A:** Maybe. I'm still pretty mad, though.

（可能吧，但是我還是很生氣。）

**B:** Yeah, but it's been a while.

（嗯，但也已經一陣子了。）

If you still don't talk to him, you might lose him.

（如果再不跟他說話，你可能會失去他。）

**A:** Oh, all right. I guess I'll call him tomorrow.

（也對，我想我明天會打給他吧。）

**When will Mary call John?**

（瑪莉何時會打電話給約翰？）

(A) Tonight.

(B) Tomorrow.

(C) Next week.

(D) Tuesday.

***Answer: (B)***

▶ Treasure is not always a friend, but a friend is always a treasure.

--Bacon

（財富不是永恆的朋友，朋友才是永恆的財富。）

--Bacon

MP3-04（稍慢速度）
MP3-23（正常速度）

**A:** Happy birthday, Mary.

（瑪莉，生日快樂。）

**B:** Thanks.

（謝謝。）

**A:** Did you get a lot of presents from your parents?

（你爸媽有給你很多生日禮物嗎？）

**B:** Nope. I just got one big present.

（沒有，我只收到一份大禮物。）

**A:** Well, what did you get?

（嗯，那你拿到的是什麼？）

**B:** I got a new car. A Toyota Camry.

（我拿到一部車子，豐田 CAMRY。）

It's really nice.
（很不錯喔。）

**What present did Mary get for her birthday?**
（瑪莉的生日禮物是什麼？）

(A) A bicycle.

(B) A pony.

(C) A Toyota Camry.

(D) A Revlon make-up kit.

***Answer: (C)***

▶Reading makes a full man, conference a ready man, and writing an exact man.

--Bacon

（閱讀使人充實，交談使人機智，寫作使人精確。）

--Bacon

# Dialogue

MP3-04（稍慢速度）
MP3-23（正常速度）

**A:** What are you up to, John?

（約翰，你在做什麼呢？）

**B:** Oh, just doing a little studying for school.

（噢，沒什麼，就是一些學校的作業。）

**A:** From the web page that's on your screen, I take it you're studying cars?

（從你螢幕上的網頁看來，我猜你在研究汽車吧。）

What class is that for?
（是什麼課要用的呢？）

**B:** Oh, well, I got a little distracted.

（噢，我有點分心了。）

That's all the Internet is good for, distractions.
（網路真的很容易讓人分心。）

**A:** I know what you mean.

（我了解你的意思。）

**What was John doing on the Internet?**

（約翰在 Internet 上做什麼？）

(A) He was studying for school.

(B) He was making web pages.

(C) He was looking for a job.

(D) He was surfing for the car pages.

***Answer: (D)***

▶It never will rain roses. When we want to have more roses we must plant trees.

---George Eliot

（天上永遠不會掉下玫瑰來，如果想要更多的玫瑰，必須自己種植。）

---- 喬治 · 艾略特

MP3-04（稍慢速度）
MP3-23（正常速度）

**A:** What are you doing on your computer, Mary?

（你在電腦上做什麼呢，瑪莉？）

**B:** What I usually do on here, chat.

（做我通常在電腦上做的事，聊天。）

**A:** What do you chat about on there all the time?

（你都在聊些什麼啊？）

**B:** Stuff.

（就是一些事情。）

**A:** Stuff? What kind of stuff?

（事情，什麼事情啊？）

**B:** You know, stuff about boys.

（你知道嘛，就是討論男生的事情囉。）

**What does Mary usually do with her computer?**
（瑪莉最常用電腦做什麼呢？）

(A) Play games.

(B) Chat about boys.

(C) Study.

(D) Surf.

***Answer: (B)***

▶Time is a bird for ever on the wing.

---T.W.Robertson

（時間是一只永遠在飛翔的鳥。）

----T・W・ 羅伯遜

# Dialogue

MP3-04（稍慢速度）
MP3-23（正常速度）

**A:** John, do you know who killed Pompeii?

（約翰你知道是誰殺了旁培？）

**B:** I'm sorry, could you repeat the question, ma'am.

（老師抱歉，你可不可以再說一次問題。）

I didn't catch it.
（我沒聽清楚。）

**A:** I think you did, John.

（我認為你聽清楚了。）

Did you study at all?
（你到底有沒有唸書啊？）

**B:** Yes, ma'am, of course I studied.

（老師，我當然有念啊。）

I just can't remember it all.
（只是沒有全部記得。）

**What does the teacher ask John?**

（老師問約翰什麼？）

(A) Who killed Julius Caesar?

(B) Who killed Marc Antony?

(C) Who killed Pompeii?

(D) Who led the revolt of the slaves in ancient Rome?

***Answer: (C)***

▶He that knows little soon repeats it.

---Western Proverb

（知識淺薄者，很快就會重覆他所知的話題。）

---- 西方諺語

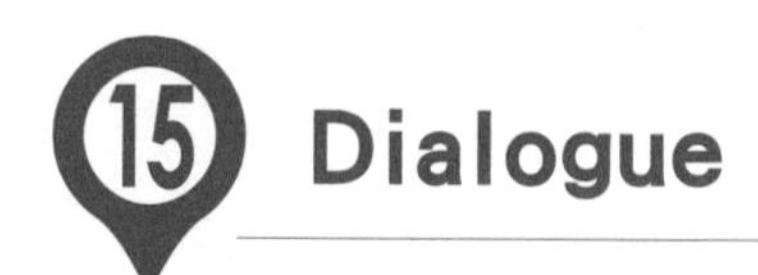


MP3-04（稍慢速度）
MP3-23（正常速度）

**A:** Hey, what's the team cheering about?

（咦，我們隊在歡呼什麼啊？）

**B:** We won, man, we won.

（我們贏了！我們贏了！）

**A:** How'd we win?

（我們怎麼贏的啊？）

We were down when I went to the restroom.

（我去廁所的時候，我們還落後啊。）

**B:** Paul made a goal right when you left, then Mark made another goal with one second left in the game.

（你離開時保羅進了一球，然後比賽結束前一秒馬克再進一球。）

We beat those French scum at last!

（我們終於打敗那些法國佬了。）

They won't win the World Cup this year.
（他們今年世界盃別想贏了。）

**A:** I can't believe it.

（真不敢相信。）

No wonder everyone's cheering.
（難怪大家都在歡呼。）

**What is the team cheering about?**
（這隊在歡呼什麼呢？）

(A) The team made it to the national championships.

(B) The team just tied with the Real Madrid.

(C) The team just beat the French national team in the World Cup.

(D) The team just won the coin toss.

***Answer: (C)***

MP3-05（稍慢速度）
MP3-24（正常速度）

**A:** You hear about the Cowboys-Cardinals game that's coming on?

（你有聽說牛仔跟紅雀隊的比賽嗎？）

**B:** Yeah. Do you know when it's on?

（有啊，你知道什麼時候開始嗎？）

**A:** Yeah, kick-off starts at 6:00 tonight.

（嗯，就是今晚六點喔。）

Everyone's meeting over at my place.
（大家都會去我那裡。）

**B:** Is that an invite?

（這算是個邀約嗎？）

**A:** As long as you bring some Buffalo Wings.

（只要你帶些辣雞翅來就成了。）

**B:** It's on.

（沒問題。）

**When are they going to watch the game?**

（他們何時要看比賽呢？）

(A) Four o’clock.

(B) Monday night.

(C) Tonight at six.

(D) Sunday afternoon.

***Answer: (C)***

# Dialogue

MP3-05（稍慢速度）
MP3-24（正常速度）

**A:** So, do you want to meet to do this homework or not?

（你想要一起做家庭作業嗎？）

**B:** Yeah, I think it would be a good idea to go over this together.

（好啊，我覺得一起做是個好主意。）

**A:** When do you want to meet?

（那你想要約什麼時候呢？）

**B:** Is Sunday afternoon good for you?

（禮拜天下午你方便嗎？）

**A:** Not really, that's family day.

（不太方便，那是我們的家庭日。）

I was kind of hoping we could do it Saturday afternoon.

（我希望跟你約星期六下午。）

**B:** Yeah, I guess that'll do.

（好啊，我應該可以）

**When are they going to meet?**

（他們相約何時見面呢？）

(A) Sunday afternoon.

(B) Saturday morning.

(C) Sunday morning.

(D) Saturday afternoon.

***Answer: (D)***

►If well used, books are the best of all things;

---R.W.Emerson

（如果利用得當，書籍就是最好的朋友。）

---R・W・ 愛默生

MP3-05（稍慢速度）
MP3-24（正常速度）

**A:** Where did you and Mike go?

（你和麥克去哪裡了呢？）

**B:** We went to watch a movie.

（我們去看電影。）

**A:** Oh? What kind of movie?

（歐，什麼電影啊？）

**B:** A horror. It was really intense, and Mike let me hold him for all the scary parts.

（恐怖片，真的很緊張，在恐怖的鏡頭時麥克都讓我握著他的手。）

**A:** Which movie was it?

（是哪部片子啊？）

**B:** The Village. It was a great movie.

（村莊，真是部很不錯的電影。）

Question 問題

**What kind of movie did they see?**
（他們去看了什麼電影？）

(A) Comedy.

(B) Sci-fi.

(C) Horror.

(D) Drama.

***Answer: (C)***

▶The reading of all good books is like a conversation with the finest men of past centuries.

---Rene Descartes

（讀好書，如同與先哲們交談。）

-- 雷內 ‧ 笛卡爾

MP3-05（稍慢速度）
MP3-24（正常速度）

**A:** Do you like horror movies?

（你喜歡看恐怖片嗎？）

**B:** Not really, but The Village was a pretty good flick.

（不是很喜歡，不過村莊真的是一部不錯的片子。）

**A:** Yeah, I didn't think you were the horror type, Mary.

（嗯，瑪莉，我不認為你是會喜歡看恐怖片的那種人。）

**B:** True, I prefer Romantic Comedies.

（沒錯，我比較喜歡浪漫喜劇。）

**A:** Just like a girl.

（就像女生一樣。）

**B:** Well, I am a girl.

（嗯，我本來就是女生啊。）

**What kind of movie does Mary like?**

（瑪莉喜歡哪種電影？）

(A) Romantic Comedy.

(B) Sci-fi.

(C) Thriller.

(D) Drama.

***Answer: (A)***

►Chance favors the minds that are prepared.

---Pasteur

（機會只願意惠顧時刻做好準備的人。）

-- 巴斯德

MP3-05（稍慢速度）
MP3-24（正常速度）

**A:** I just wanted it to be over, but when it finally ended, I was kind of sad.

（我本來希望它結束的，但真的結束時，我又覺得有點難過。）

**B:** Why were you sad?

（你為什麼難過？）

**A:** Well, we were out there, playing our horns, marching, doing the best we could, and we didn't win the band contest.

（嗯，我們在那裡演奏小號，遊行，全力以赴，結果還是沒有贏得樂團比賽。）

**B:** I'm sorry you didn't win.

（真遺憾你們沒贏。）

**A:** That's okay.

（沒關係啦。）

Even though we were disappointed with the outcome, it was exhilarating to see everyone cheering for us in the stadium.
（雖然我們對結果很失望，但看到大家在體育場為我們加油，還是覺得很興奮。）

**B:** Oh yeah?

（真的嗎？）

**A:** Yeah, it was a lot of fun.

（嗯，真的很有趣。）

**What are they talking about?**
（他們在討論什麼？）

(A) A motocross competition.

(B) A band contest.

(C) A chess match.

(D) The football game last night.

***Answer: (B)***

# Dialogue

MP3-06（稍慢速度）
MP3-25（正常速度）

**A:** You didn't come here to the airport to stop me from getting on that plane, did you, Mary?

（瑪莉，你來機場不是想阻止我上飛機吧？）

**B:** No, I came here to tell you that I love you, John.

（不是，我來只是告訴你我愛你，約翰。）

But you can go ahead and leave.
（但是，你還是可以走。）

Just remember what I told you.
（只是要記得我跟你說的話。）

**A:** I'm confused.

（我覺得很疑惑。）

So you want me to go?
（你希望我走嗎？）

**B:** No, I don't want you to go.

（不，我不希望你走。）

I'm just not going to tell you what to do.
（我只是不會跟你說你該怎麼做。）

**A:** But if you love me

（但是如果你愛我）

**B:** And I do.

（我是愛你啊。）

**A:** Then you would want me to stay.

（那你應該希望我留下來啊。）

Well, I love you too, and so I think I will stay.
（嗯，我也愛你，我想我會留下來。）

**What does Mary come to the airport for?**
（瑪莉為什麼來機場？）

(A) To tell John goodbye.

(B) To stop John from going.

(C) To tell John she loves him.

(D) To go with John to Florida.

***Answer: (C)***

# Dialogue

MP3-06（稍慢速度）
MP3-25（正常速度）

**A:** What were you doing out in the yard?

（你在院子裡做什麼？）

**B:** I just had to finish planting.

（我必須把植物種完。）

I planted three more flowers.
（我剛又種了三棵花。）

**A:** On top of the six you planted this morning?

（除了你今天早上種的那六棵嗎？）

**B:** Yup.

（是啊。）

**A:** And the dozen you planted yesterday?

（還有你昨天種的十二朵？）

**B:** That's right.

（是的。）

And I'm finally done.
（終於種完了。）

**How many flowers did Mary plant totally?**

（瑪莉總共種了多少花？）

(A) 9

(B) 21

(C) 8

(D) 25

***Answer: (B)***

# Dialogue

MP3-06（稍慢速度）
MP3-25（正常速度）

**A:** Hey John, where have you been?

（嗨，約翰，你剛去哪裡？）

**B:** I just got back from the zoo.

（我剛從動物園回來。）

**A:** Oh, yeah? How was it?

（真的嗎？好玩嗎？）

**B:** It was awesome.

（棒極了。）

The monkey exhibit there was sweet.
（猴子展覽好可愛喔。）

I must have seen sixty monkeys.
（我大概看到了六十隻猴子。）

**A:** Sixty monkeys?

（六十隻猴子？）

**B:** At least!

（嗯，至少！）

**How many monkeys did John see in the zoo?**
（約翰在動物園看到多少隻猴子？）

(A) As many as sixty monkeys.

(B) No more than sixty monkeys.

(C) Possibly more than sixty monkeys.

(D) Exactly sixty monkeys.

***Answer: (C)***

▶Life is a sweet and joyful thing for one who has a pure conscience.

---Leo Tolstoy

（心靈純淨的人，人生充滿著甜蜜和喜悅。）

-- 列夫 ・ 托爾斯泰

# Dialogue

MP3-06（稍慢速度）
MP3-25（正常速度）

**A:** Hey John, why are you so glum?

（嗨，約翰，怎麼那麼悶悶不樂呢？）

**B:** Mary just left me.

（瑪莉離開我了。）

**A:** What, like, she went to the grocery store?

（什麼，你是說她去雜貨店嗎？）

**B:** No, she dumped me.

（不是，她把我甩了。）

She's moving out her stuff.
（她正在把她的東西搬出去。）

**A:** Oh, I'm sorry.

（噢，我很難過。）

**B:** Yeah, well, it's not your fault. Or is it?

（嗯，這不是你的錯啦，或者其實是？）

**Why does John seem unhappy?**
（約翰為什麼不開心呢？）

(A) The neighbor ran over his cat.

(B) Mary left him.

(C) The neighbor ran over his dog.

(D) His best friend died.

***Answer: (B)***

▶He that knows little soon repeats it.

---Western Proverb

（知識淺薄者，很快就會重覆他所知的話題。）

-- 西方諺語

MP3-06（稍慢速度）
MP3-25（正常速度）

**A:** I can't believe it!

（我真不敢相信！）

**B:** What? What happened, Mary?

（怎麼了？瑪莉。發生了什麼事？）

Why are you so excited?
（你怎麼這麼興奮？）

**A:** I won the contest!

（我比贏了！）

I won the car!
（我贏得一部車！）

**B:** That's pretty cool.

（太棒了！）

What are you going to do with it?
（你要怎麼處理這部車呢？）

I mean, are you going to keep it?
（我是說你要留著用嗎？）

**A:** No, I'll probably sell it.

（不會，我也許會把它賣了。）

I need the money for rent.
（我需要錢繳房租。）

**What is Mary excited about?**
（瑪莉在興奮什麼？）

(A) She aced the final exam.

(B) Paul likes her.

(C) She won a new car.

(D) She won a trip to the Bahamas.

***Answer: (C)***

# Dialogue

MP3-07（稍慢速度）
MP3-26（正常速度）

**A:** Where's the bus stop around here?

（這附近的公車站在哪裡呢？）

**B:** It's right on the corner over there.

（就在轉角那裡。）

**A:** When does it come by?

（公車多久會來一班？）

**B:** Every hour on the thirty.

（每整點三十分來。）

**A:** In the mornings and the evenings?

（早上和晚上都是嗎？）

**B:** It comes all day on the thirty.

（全天的整點三十分都會來。）

**How often does the bus run?**
（公車開車頻率如何？）

(A) Every thirty minutes.

(B) Every forty-five minutes.

(C) Every hour.

(D) Every hour and a half.

***Answer: (C)***

# Dialogue

MP3-07（稍慢速度）
MP3-26（正常速度）

**A:** Mom, would you get me a computer?

（媽，你可不可以買一台電腦給我？）

**B:** Why can't you just use your father's, Bobby?

（巴比，你為何不可以用爸爸的呢？）

**A:** But I'm going away to university, and I'll need it for classes.

（因為我要上大學了，要帶去學校用。）

**B:** You can't use your roommate's?

（你不能用你室友的嗎？）

**A:** I don't even know my roommate.

（我根本不認識我室友。）

If you want me to do well in class, you'll get me a new computer.

（如果你們希望我功課好的話，就要買一台新電腦給我們。）

**Why does Mary need a computer?**

（為什麼瑪莉需要一台電腦？）

(A) For school

(B) To use the internet

(C) To write a book

(D) To find the first five thousand digits to pi

***Answer: (A)***

▶Living without an aim is like sailing without a compass.

---Alexandre Dumas

（生活沒有目標，就像航海沒有指南針。）

MP3-07（稍慢速度）
MP3-26（正常速度）

**A:** I'm going to be late for work today.

（我今天上班要遲到了。）

**B:** Why?

（為什麼？）

**A:** Well, my car doesn't work.

（嗯，我的車子壞掉了。）

**B:** What's wrong with it?

（車子怎麼了？）

Can someone just jump it?
（沒人會修嗎？）

**A:** No, my dad says the radiator is blown.

（沒有，我爸說冷卻器壞掉了。）

**B:** Will he give you a ride?

（他會不會載你一程呢？）

**A:** He will, but like I said, we'll be a little late.

（他會，但就像我說的，會有點遲到。）

## What's the problem with Mary's car?

（瑪麗的車子怎麼了？）

(A) The alternator is out.

(B) The radiator is blown.

(C) The alignment is off.

(D) The gasket is leaking.

***Answer: (B)***

MP3-07（稍慢速度）
MP3-26（正常速度）

**A:** John, Why do you keep running off to the post office?

（約翰，你為什麼一直跑郵局呢？）

**B:** I'm expecting a package.

（我在等一個包裹。）

**A:** What's the package?

（是什麼包裹？）

**B:** It's a gift for Lisa.

（那是給麗莎的禮物。）

It's a necklace.
（一條項鍊。）

I found a really good deal on a website.
（我在網站上看到的好交易。）

**A:** You bought a necklace for Lisa on the web?

（你在網路上買了一條項鍊送麗莎？）

**B:** Yeah. You can't tell the quality of jewelry in real life anyway.

（是啊，反正就算看到實物也分辨不出珠寶的品質啊。）

**What is John expecting?**

（約翰在等什麼？）

(A) A surprise party.

(B) A kiss.

(C) A necklace.

(D) Money.

***Answer: (C)***

# 30 Dialogue

MP3-07（稍慢速度）
MP3-26（正常速度）

**A:** I am so tired.

（我好累喔。）

I stayed up so late last night.
（昨晚熬夜到好晚。）

**B:** Why did you stay up, Mary?

（瑪莉，你為何要熬夜呢？）

**A:** I was talking to John on the phone.

（我跟約翰在講電話。）

He's incredible.
（他真是太棒了）

**B:** So, do you like him?

（那麼，你喜歡他囉？）

**A:** I think so. We're going to go out on Friday.

（我想是吧，我們星期五要一起出去。）

**Why did Mary stay up last night?**

（瑪莉為何昨晚熬夜？）

(A) She was doing homework.

(B) She was talking to John on the phone.

(C) She was watching television.

(D) She was working.

***Answer: (B)***

# 31 Dialogue

MP3-08（稍慢速度）
MP3-27（正常速度）

**A:** I mean, you just cast the line in there and wait and wait.

（我是說，你把線丟下去後就開始耐心等待吧。）

**B:** The thing I hate the most about fishing is the waiting.

（我最討厭釣魚的地方就是要一直等。）

**A:** But John, I think something's biting.

（但是約翰，我覺得有東西在咬餌囉。）

John, pay attention, something's biting.
（約翰，注意，有東西在咬餌了。）

**B:** Ah, something's biting!

（有東西在咬餌了！）

Get the net!
（去把網拿過來。）

Here's the fun part.
（這就是有趣的部分。）

**What is John doing?**

（約翰在做什麼？）

(A) Hunting

(B) Fishing

(C) Playing video games

(D) Playing basketball

***Answer: (B)***

# Dialogue

MP3-08（稍慢速度）
MP3-27（正常速度）

**A:** I'm going to the store, do you need anything?

（我要去買東西。有需要什麼嗎？）

**B:** Yeah, could you bring me back some green onions?

（是的，可以幫我買一些青蔥嗎？）

**A:** You need some green onions?

（你需要些青蔥嗎？）

No problem, I'll bring you back some.

（沒問題，我會幫你買回來。）

**B:** Thanks, I appreciate it.

（謝囉，我很感激。）

**A:** It's no problem at all.

（小事情別客氣。）

**What will Mary bring back?**
（瑪莉會帶回什麼呢？）

(A) Eggs

(B) Milk

(C) Green onions

(D) Ham

***Answer: (C)***

# Dialogue

MP3-08（稍慢速度）
MP3-27（正常速度）

**A:** You're going to have to speak up!

（你要講大聲一點！）

**B:** I said, "We need to go to John's house!"

（我說：「我們必須去約翰家！」）

**A:** A little louder, the train's drowning you out!

（再大聲一點，火車的聲音蓋過你了！）

**B:** Let's get out of the station so we can talk!

（我們出站吧，這樣才能講話！）

**A:** What?

（什麼？）

**B:** I said, "Let's get out of the station so we can talk!"

（我說：「我們出站吧，這樣才能講話！」）

**Where does the conversation take place?**

（這段對話發生在哪裡？）

(A) At an airport

(B) At the museum

(C) At a bus stop

(D) At a train station

***Answer: (D)***

MP3-08（稍慢速度）
MP3-27（正常速度）

**A:** What magazine are you reading?

（你在看什麼雜誌？）

**B:** PC Life.

（電腦生活。）

**A:** Is it any good?

（好看嗎？）

**B:** Yeah, it's pretty interesting.

（對啊，很有趣。）

**A:** Why don't you get a subscription?

（你為什麼不乾脆訂閱呢？）

**B:** Well, it says here that the magazine will stop monthly publication in January.

（這裡寫著，這本雜誌一月份就要停止每月發行了。）

So what's the point?
（訂閱有什麼用？）

I'll just buy a few issues that look interesting.
（我只會買幾期看起來有趣的來看。）

**When will *PC Life* magazine stop monthly publication?**
（電腦生活雜誌何時會停止每月發行？）

(A) January

(B) February

(C) March

(D) December

***Answer: (A)***

MP3-08（稍慢速度）
MP3-27（正常速度）

**A:** I'm going to go to the grocery store.

（我要去雜貨店。）

**B:** Which one?

（哪一家？）

**A:** I'm thinking Food Lion.

（我想去獅子座食品。）

They're the cheapest, aren't they?

（那一家最便宜了，不是嗎？）

**B:** I guess so.

（我想是吧。）

They've got a good bakery at the one on the corner.

（他們在轉角處有個很棒的烘培店。）

Would you get me some French bread?

（你可以幫我買些法國麵包嗎？）

**A:** Sure.

（沒問題。）

**What is *Food Lion*?**

（獅子座食品是什麼？）

(A) A movie

(B) A book

(C) A ship

(D) A grocery store

***Answer: (D)***

# 36 Dialogue

MP3-09（稍慢速度）
MP3-28（正常速度）

**A:** Dude, check out the label on the can.

（喂，看一看罐頭上的標籤吧。）

**B:** What about it?

（怎麼了？）

**A:** It says, "Can will explode at 120 degrees".

（它說：「罐子在 120 度會爆炸。」）

**B:** Yeah, so?

（歐，真的嗎？）

**A:** Why does it need to say that?

（為什麼要說這個呢？）

Would there be anyone who is dumb enough to heat the can so that it would explode?

（有哪個笨蛋會把罐子弄那麼熱，然後讓它爆炸呢？）

**B:** I guess.

（應該沒有人會那樣吧。）

**A:** Well you want to try?

（咦，你不會想試試看吧？）

**At what temperature will the can explode?**

（這個罐子幾度會爆炸呢？）

(A) 100 degrees

(B) 120 degrees

(C) 130 degrees

(D) 150 degrees

***Answer: (B)***

## Dialogue

MP3-09（稍慢速度）
MP3-28（正常速度）

**A:** Where are you going for spring break?

（你春假要去哪裡？）

**B:** I'm going on a cruise.

（我要去參加一個航行。）

**A:** What's the ship called?

（船名叫什麼？）

**B:** The Mary Queen.

（瑪莉皇后號。）

**A:** How long is the cruise?

（要航行多久？）

**B:** For a week and a half.

（一週半。）

**A:** But spring break is only for a week?

（但是春假只有一週？）

**B:** Well, I guess I'll have to miss some of school.

（嗯，我大概會翹幾堂課吧。）

**What is *Mary Queen*?**

（瑪莉皇后號是什麼？）

(A) A dog

(B) A cat

(C) A church

(D) A ship

***Answer: (D)***

# Dialogue

MP3-09（稍慢速度）
MP3-28（正常速度）

**A:** So you're going to be on Mary Queen for a week and a half?

（那麼你要在瑪莉皇后號船上待一週半？）

**B:** You bet. It should be pretty fun.

（沒錯，一定很有趣。）

**A:** What's the route?

（路線如何？）

**B:** It sails from Miami to Cozumel and then back, stopping at a couple of islands along the way.

（從邁阿密到寇茲梅然後折返，一陸上停靠幾個小島。）

**A:** Sounds pretty fun.

（聽起來真的很不錯。）

**Where does *Mary Queen* sail from?**

（瑪莉皇后號從哪裡啟航？）

(A) Miami, FL

(B) New Orleans, LA

(C) Corpus Christi, TX

(D) Galveston, TX

***Answer: (A)***

# 39 Dialogue

MP3-09（稍慢速度）
MP3-28（正常速度）

**A:** That was the longest drive I've ever been on.

（這真是我最長的一次開車了。）

**B:** Yeah, but we're finally here in New York.

（是啊，我們終於到紐約了。）

**A:** I just hope we can find a hotel.

（我只希望能找到間飯店。）

**B:** Is that all you can think about?

（你能想到的就是這些？）

**A:** After driving three days straight, you bet that's all I can think about.

（連續開了三天車，當然我只能想到這個。）

My back hurts.
（我的背很痛。）

I need a bed. And a drink.
（我需要床和飲料。）

**B:** I'll second you on the drink.
（我贊成去喝飲料。）

**How long did they take to get to New York?**
（他們花了多久的時間到達紐約？）

(A) A month

(B) Two weeks

(C) One week

(D) Three days

***Answer: (D)***

MP3-09（稍慢速度）
MP3-28（正常速度）

**A:** That was one of the coolest train rides I've ever taken.

（這真是我最棒的一次搭火車經驗。）

**B:** From Paris to London, under the English Channel via the Chunnel, you bet it was.

（從巴黎到倫敦，經由英法隧道穿越英吉利海峽，當然很棒囉。）

That's something to brag about.
（那是值得大肆吹噓的一件事。）

**A:** It wasn't too long, either.

（而且也不會太久。）

I thought it would be longer.
（我以為會更久一些。）

**B:** It's high speed train, of course it was fast.

（這是高速火車，速度當然很快。）

## How did they get to London?

（他們怎麼到倫敦的？）

(A) By airplane

(B) By car

(C) By train

(D) By ship

***Answer: (C)***

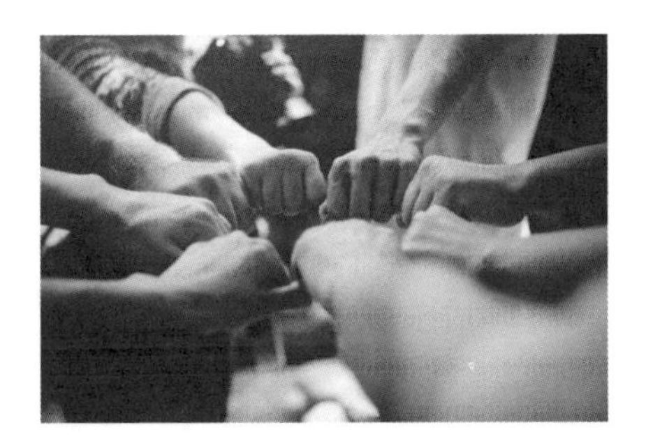

MP3-10（稍慢速度）
MP3-29（正常速度）

**A:** What movie did you rent?

（你租了什麼片子？）

**B:** 50 First Dates. Have you seen it yet?

（前 50 個約會。你有看過嗎？）

**A:** No, not yet.

（還沒。）

How long do you have it for?
（你的租期有多久？）

**B:** It's due back on Tuesday.

（星期二要還回。）

You want me to wait, so you can watch it?
（你要我等等，讓你看這部片嗎？）

**A:** Yeah, would you?

（是啊，你會這麼做嗎？）

**B:** No problem.

（沒問題。）

**When is the movie due back?**

（片子何時要歸還？）

(A) Monday

(B) Tuesday

(C) Wednesday

(D) Friday

***Answer: (B)***

MP3-10（稍慢速度）
MP3-29（正常速度）

**A:** Can you figure out this commercial?

（你看得懂這個廣告嗎？）

It's so bizarre.
（好奇特喔。）

**B:** Oh, it's a Coca-cola commercial.

（嗯，這是可口可樂的廣告。）

**A:** How do you know?

（你怎知道？）

**B:** Well, everyone's holding a can of Coke, for one thing.

（一方面是因為每個人手上都拿著可樂。）

**A:** Yeah, I guess they are.

（對，我想他們確實是如此。）

It really isn't focused on though.
（不過並沒有很強調。）

**B:** It's supposed to be subliminal.

（應該是下意識的感覺吧。）

**What's that advertising?**

（這是什麼廣告？）

(A) Pepsi

(B) Coca-cola

(C) Fruit of the Loom

(D) Levi's

***Answer: (B)***

MP3-10（稍慢速度）
MP3-29（正常速度）

**A:** Did you drive this morning?

（你今早有開車嗎？）

**B:** No, why? Was the traffic bad?

（沒，怎麼了，交通很糟嗎？）

**A:** It was hideous.

（很恐怖。）

It was backed up for miles.
（回堵數英里。）

**B:** Why?

（怎麼會這樣呢？）

**A:** I think there was a wreck.

（我覺得是有交通事故。），

But by the time I got off the freeway, it was still bumper to bumper.
（但當我下交流道時，還是很擠。）

I never got to see what caused the jam.
（我不知道為什麼交通會塞成這樣。）

**How was traffic that morning?**
（今早的交通如何？）

(A) Pleasant

(B) Fine

(C) Very bad

(D) Pretty smooth

***Answer: (C)***

# 44 Dialogue

MP3-10（稍慢速度）
MP3-29（正常速度）

**A:** I'm getting kind of bored of this video game.

（我對這個遊樂器越來越厭煩了。）

**B:** Well, what do you want to do then?

（嗯，那你想做什麼呢？）

**A:** How about going to shoot some hoops?

（我們去打籃球好嗎？）

**B:** Yeah, sure, why not?

（嗯，好啊，有何不可？）

**What will they probably do next?**
（他們等下可能去做什麼？）

(A) Shoot pool

(B) Play cards

(C) Watch television

(D) Play basketball

***Answer: (D)***

MP3-10（稍慢速度）
MP3-29（正常速度）

**A:** This website is so sweet.

（這個網站真棒。）

**B:** Do you really think so?

（你真這樣覺得？）

**A:** Yeah. Who designed it?

（是啊，是誰設計的呢？）

**B:** I did.

（是我設計的。）

**A:** You did, John?

（約翰，是你設計的？）

**B:** Yeah, I do websites on the side.

（是的，我業餘時有在做網站。）

**Who designed the website?**
（這網站是誰設計的？）

(A) Veritas Web Publishing

(B) John

(C) Luke

(D) Mark

***Answer: (B)***

MP3-11（稍慢速度）
MP3-30（正常速度）

**A:** Mary, would you go research this for me?

（瑪莉，可以請你幫我做這個研究嗎？）

**B:** Didn't I assign this part of the project to you?

（我不是已經把企劃的這部分派你做了嗎？）

**A:** Yeah, but it's not the entire part that you assigned,,,

（是啊，但這些又不是你派給我的全部）

**B:** The point though, John, is that you shouldn't be asking me to do anything.

（約翰，重點是，你不該要求我做任何東西。）

Who's in charge of the project? Me or you?
（到底是你還是我在負責這個計劃啊？）

**A:** You are, Mary, you are.

（當然是你啊，瑪莉。）

Fine, I'll get Fred to do it.

（好吧，我去叫佛烈德做吧。）

**Who's in charge of the project, Mary or John?**

**（誰負責這個計劃，瑪莉還是約翰？）**

(A) Mary

(B) John

***Answer: (A)***

MP3-11（稍慢速度）
MP3-30（正常速度）

**A:** Hey, Fred, did you get the message about the party for John's birthday?

（嗨，佛烈德，你有聽說約翰的生日派對嗎？）

**B:** No, Jack, I didn't.

（我沒聽說，傑克。）

**A:** Well, it's at Mary's house on Saturday.

（嗯，星期六在瑪莉家舉行。）

Don't tell John, it's a surprise.
（不要告訴約翰喔，要讓他驚喜一下。）

**B:** What time do I come over?

（我什麼時候該到呢？）

**A:** Sometime before 7:00, that's when we're planning on getting him to get to Mary's.

（七點前到吧，我們打算那時讓他到瑪莉家。）

**Whose surprise party are they planning for?**
（他們在幫誰計劃驚喜派對？）

(A) John's

(B) Mary's

(C) Fred's

(D) Jack's

***Answer: (A)***

MP3-11（稍慢速度）
MP3-30（正常速度）

**A:** So, we were waiting for John to get to Mary's for about an hour.

（我們等約翰到瑪莉家，等了快一個小時。）

He didn't get there until 8:00.
（他到八點才來。）

I didn't know what to do with all the guests for so long.
（我都不知道該怎麼對滿座的賓客交代。）

**B:** Why was John late?

（約翰為什麼遲到呢？）

**A:** Apparently he and Mary had a fight.

（很明顯的，他跟瑪莉吵了一架。）

And then Mary finally gave in – an hour later – and she finally brought him over.
（終於在一個小時後，瑪莉投降了，然後把他帶來了。）

**B:** Why did they have a fight?

（他們在吵什麼呢？）

**A:** Something about John teasing her about the dress making her look fat.

（約翰笑她，說她穿的衣服讓她看起來很胖。）

**Why was John late?**

（約翰為何遲到？）

(A) The play he and Mary went to watch started late.

(B) It took forever for the waiter to bring them their food at the restaurant.

(C) John and Mary got in a car wreck.

(D) John and Mary got in a fight.

***Answer: (D)***

MP3-11（稍慢速度）
MP3-30（正常速度）

**A:** What did you do last weekend?

（你週末做了什麼呢？）

**B:** I hunted some deer.

（我去獵了些鹿。）

**A:** Where at?

（在哪裡獵的？）

**B:** We went to Broken Bow State Park, up in Oklahoma.

（我們往北到奧克拉荷馬州的布羅肯波州立公園獵的。）

**A:** Oh yeah? Who did you go with?

（真的嗎，跟誰一起去的？）

**B:** Peter and Sam. It was pretty fun.

（跟彼得和山姆，真的很好玩。）

**Where did John hunt deer?**
（約翰在哪裡獵鹿？）

(A) Broken Bow State Park

(B) Beaver's Bend State Park

(C) Broken Arrow State Park

(D) Robber's Cave State Park

***Answer: (A)***

▶ The horizonog life is broadened chiefly by the enlargement of the heart.

---H. Blade

（生生活的視野主要是是隨著心胸的開闊而變得寬廣。）

MP3-11（稍慢速度）
MP3-30（正常速度）

**A:** So, Mary, when do you graduate?

（瑪莉，你何時畢業？）

**B:** This May.

（今年五月。）

**A:** Do you know what you want to do?

（你知道你想做什麼嗎？）

**B:** Not really.

（還不太確定。）

I'm going Europe in the summer, though.
（我暑假會先去歐洲），

Then, I don't know.
（然後也沒什麼計劃。）

Maybe go back to school; maybe go to work.
（也許會再去唸書，也許會去工作。）

**A:** Europe sounds fun.

（歐洲聽起來不錯喔。）

**B:** You're welcome to come if you'd like.

（如果你喜歡的話，歡迎你來喔。）

**Where is Mary going after she graduates?**

**（瑪莉畢業後想去哪裡呢？）**

(A) Go back to university.

(B) Europe.

(C) Work at a marketing firm.

(D) New York.

***Answer: (B)***

MP3-12（稍慢速度）
MP3-31（正常速度）

**A:** I feel like sailing.

（我想去坐帆船。）

**B:** Well, why don't you?

（那怎不去呢？）

**A:** I don't have a sail boat, or anyone to go with.

（我沒有帆船，也沒有人陪我去。）

**B:** I'd go with you, if you asked.

（如果你要求，我可以跟你一起去。）

**A:** You really want to go?

（你真的想去嗎？）

**B:** Of course, it'd be fun.

（當然囉，應該會很好玩。）

Foreword 前言

第一部分 聽力測驗問題

第二部分 聽力測驗解答

**A:** What are we going to do about not having a sailboat?

（沒有帆船我們要怎麼辦呢？）

**B:** We could always rent one at the marina.

（我們在碼頭租一艘就好了。）

**What should people do if they want to sail?**

（如果想坐帆船，應該怎麼做呢？）

(A) Rent a sailboat

(B) Steal a sailboat

(C) Go fishing

(D) Borrow a sailboat from someone at the dock

***Answer: (A)***

# Dialogue

MP3-12（稍慢速度）
MP3-31（正常速度）

**A:** Hello. Is Mary there?

（哈囉，瑪莉在嗎？）

**B:** I'm sorry, Mary can't come to the phone.

（抱歉，瑪莉現在不方便接電話。）

**A:** What? Is there something wrong?

（怎麼了，有什麼問題嗎？）

**B:** She isn't feeling very well.

（她身體不太舒服。）

**A:** Ah, well, tell her Steve said to get well.

（歐，那請轉告她，史帝夫祝她早日康復。）

**What's wrong with Mary?**

（瑪莉怎麼了？）

(A) She failed her test.

(B) She broke up with her boyfriend.

(C) She's sick.

(D) She lost all of her money gambling.

***Answer: (C)***

MP3-12（稍慢速度）
MP3-31（正常速度）

**A:** What's the deal with John?

（約翰怎麼了？）

He seems pretty upset.
（看起來心情很不好。）

**B:** He just lost his job.

（他剛丟了工作。）

**A:** What for?

（為什麼？）

**B:** The boss was yelling at him and he lost his temper.

（老闆對他大聲，結果他就失控了。）

**A:** And he lost his job for that?

（就這樣丟了工作嗎？）

**B:** Well, he lost his temper and hit the boss.

（嗯，他失控了，還打他老闆。）

**What's wrong with John?**

（約翰怎麼了？）

(A) He's sick.

(B) He lost his job.

(C) He lost his money gambling.

(D) He got lost on the freeway.

***Answer: (B)***

MP3-12（稍慢速度）
MP3-31（正常速度）

**A:** I hear you're going to Europe, Mrs. Lin.

（林太太，我聽說你要去歐洲。）

**B:** I sure am, right after school gets out.

（是啊，學校一結束就去。）

**A:** Do you have everything set?

（東西都準備好了嗎？）

**B:** Yes. I even got a belt to hold my passport and wallet.

（是啊，我還買了一條腰帶，裝我的護照和錢包呢。）

**A:** What for?

（為什麼呢？）

**B:** So the gypsies won't steal my passport or money.

（這樣吉普賽人就偷不到我的護照和錢了。）

**What is Mrs. Lin worried about?**
（林太太擔心什麼？）

(A) A train wreck

(B) A plane crash

(C) Getting killed

(D) Gypsies

***Answer: (D)***

MP3-12（稍慢速度）
MP3-31（正常速度）

**A:** Hey, listen to this recording I made.

（嗨，來聽聽我錄的東西。）

**B:** What's it for, John?

（約翰，是什麼啊？）

**A:** My voicemail. Isn't it funny?

（我的語音信箱，很好玩吧？）

**B:** I think it's kind of annoying, actually.

（事實上，我覺得很難聽。），

It makes me not want to leave you a voicemail.

（讓我不想留話給你。）

**A:** That's the point.

（這就是了。）

**Where is the recorded message most likely to be heard?**
（這個錄音最有可能出現在哪裡？）

(A) On an answering machine.

(B) On the television.

(C) On the radio.

(D) On John's voicemail.

***Answer: (D)***

MP3-13（稍慢速度）
MP3-32（正常速度）

**A:** What are you ordering to eat?

（你要點什麼吃？）

**B:** I think I'll get the pizza.

（我想要點個披薩。）

**A:** I don't like pizza.
（我不喜歡披薩。）

**B:** Well, I like it. How about you?

（嗯，我喜歡，那你要什麼呢？）

**A:** I think I'll settle for spaghetti with meat balls.

（我想那就點個肉丸義大利麵吧。）

**Where does the conversation possibly take place?**

（這個對話最有可能在哪裡發生？）

(A) On a train car.

(B) At a restaurant.

(C) At someone's house.

(D) At work.

***Answer: (B)***

## 57 Dialogue

MP3-13（稍慢速度）
MP3-32（正常速度）

**A:** Why are we so early?

（我們為什麼這麼早呢？）

**B:** So we could get a ticket for a good seat.

（這樣我們才能買到好位子的票啊。）

**A:** But the show doesn't come on for another three hours!

（但是表演還要再三個小時才開始！）

**B:** Well, if we came later, we wouldn't get as good a seat.

（嗯，如果我們太晚到，就沒辦法拿到好位子啊。）

**A:** If we were any earlier, this place wouldn't be open yet!

（如果再早一點，那這邊就根本還沒開！）

**When does the show come on?**
（表演還要多久才開始？）

(A) In one hour.

(B) In two hours.

(C) In three hours.

(D) In four hours.

***Answer: (C)***

MP3-13（稍慢速度）
MP3-32（正常速度）

**A:** Hey John! Are you going to race today?

（嘿，約翰！你今天要去賽跑嗎？）

**B:** Hey Paul.

（嗨，保羅。）

No, I sprained my ankle earlier this week, so I won't be able to race for a while.
（我不去，因為我這週腳踝扭傷了，一陣子不能賽跑了。）

**A:** Ah, then no point in watching the competition today, eh?

（那今天的比賽就沒看頭了嗎？）

**B:** Not so, Roger will be competing.

（不盡然，羅杰會參加比賽。）

He's pretty fast and fun to watch.
（他跑得很快，觀賽會很有趣。）

**Who is going to be racing?**
（誰要參加賽跑？）

(A) Paul

(B) Roger

(C) John

(D) Mark

***Answer: (B)***

MP3-13（稍慢速度）
MP3-32（正常速度）

**A:** I can't believe it!

（我真不敢相信。）

Roger was racing Mark and Mark won?
（羅傑和馬克賽跑，而馬克贏了？）

Roger is so much better than Mark.
（羅傑比馬克強很多。）

I know, I was thinking that Roger would win, too.
（對啊，我也以為羅傑會贏。）

**A:** Maybe Mark cheated somehow?

（也許馬克有作弊喔？）

**B:** Now, now, just because he won doesn't mean he cheated.

（這個嘛，不能因為他贏就說他是作弊啊。）

## Who won the race?
（誰贏了比賽？）

(A) John

(B) Paul

(C) Roger

(D) Mark

***Answer: (D)***

MP3-13（稍慢速度）
MP3-32（正常速度）

**A:** What's the weather going to be like today?

（今天天氣會如何呢？）

**B:** 80 percent chance of rain.

（百分之八十的降雨機會。）

**A:** More rain?

（還要下雨？）

It's been raining for four days already.
（已經下四天了。）

**B:** No kidding.

（是沒錯。）

But just when it stops, we'll be complaining that we don't get enough rain.
（但當雨停時，我們又會抱怨沒有足夠的雨水。）

**A:** True, true.

（正是如此。）

**How many days has it been raining?**

（已經下幾天雨了？）

(A) 1 day

(B) 2 days

(C) 3 days

(D) 4 days

***Answer: (D)***

MP3-14（稍慢速度）
MP3-33（正常速度）

**A:** What's the weather supposed to be like this weekend?

（本週的天氣會怎樣呢？）

**B:** It's supposed to snow.

（應該會下雪吧。）

**A:** I hate snow.

（我討厭雪。）

Are you sure that's what it's supposed to do?

（你確定是這樣嗎？）

**B:** That's what they said this morning.

（他們今天早上是這麼說的。）

**A:** Hopefully they're wrong.

（希望他們是錯的。）

**Does John like snow?**
（約翰喜歡雪嗎？）

(A) He hates it.

(B) His ambivalent toward it.

(C) He likes it.

(D) He loves it.

***Answer: (A)***

MP3-14（稍慢速度）
MP3-33（正常速度）

**A:** What should we do for winter break?

（我們寒假要做什麼呢？）

**B:** John said we should go to his place in Vancouver.

（約翰說我們應該去溫哥華找他。）

**A:** What would we do there?

（去那裡要做什麼呢？）

**B:** We'd go skiing.

（我們可以去滑雪。）

He's got a house right on the slopes.

（他在山坡上有棟房子。）

**A:** Sounds good to me.

（聽起來不錯喔。）

**What are they going to do?**
（他們要去做什麼？）

(A) Go to the Bahamas.

(B) Go skiing in Vancouver.

(C) Go skiing in Colorado.

(D) Go to California.

***Answer: (B)***

MP3-14（稍慢速度）
MP3-33（正常速度）

**A:** Hey John, where do you think we should go to eat?

（嗨，約翰，你覺得我們該去哪裡吃東西呢？）

**B:** Why not the Tokyo House?

（何不去東京屋？）

**A:** Sounds good to me.

（聽起來不錯。）

Do they have sushi there?
（他們有壽司嗎？）

**B:** Among other things, yes.

（不但有壽司，其他的也有。）

**Where does John recommend them to go?**
（約翰建議他們去哪裡？）

(A) Tokyo House

(B) Kim Long Chinese & Vietnamese Buffet

(C) Jack's Steakhouse

(D) Macaroni Grill

***Answer: (A)***

# 64 Dialogue

MP3-14（稍慢速度）
MP3-33（正常速度）

**A:** Hey John. Where have you been?

（嗨，約翰，你去哪裡了？）

**B:** Oh, I didn't tell you?

（喔，我沒告訴你嗎？）

I went to Vegas last week.
（我上週去拉斯維加斯。）

**A:** Awesome. Did you win anything?

（太棒了，有贏回什麼東西嗎？）

**B:** Win? No, but I lost three hundred bucks.

（並沒有贏，倒是輸掉三百元。）

**A:** I'm sorry.

（太可惜了。）

**B:** Don't be.

（還好啦。）

It was fun.
（很好玩就是了。）

**Where did John go last week?**
（約翰上週去哪裡？）

(A) San Diego, CA

(B) Las Vegas, NV

(C) Dallas, TX

(D) Tulsa, OK

***Answer: (B)***

MP3-14（稍慢速度）
MP3-33（正常速度）

**A:** How was your trip to the Bahamas, Mary?

（瑪莉，你的巴哈馬之旅如何啊？）

**B:** It was fantastic. I loved the place.

（很棒啊，我愛死那個地方了。）

**A:** Oh, yeah?

（真的嗎？）

**B:** Yeah. There were hot guys everywhere.

（對啊，到處都有帥哥喔。）

**A:** Are you going to go again anytime soon?

（你很快又想再去嗎？）

**B:** I'm thinking next year.

（嗯，明年吧。）

**Did Mary enjoy her trip?**

（瑪莉玩的開心嗎？）

(A) Yes

(B) No

***Answer: (A)***

► A man can succeed at almost anything for which he has unlimited enthusiasm.

---Charles Schwab

（一個人只要他有無限的熱情，就幾乎可以在任何事情上取得成功。）

# 66 Dialogue

MP3-15（稍慢速度）
MP3-34（正常速度）

**A:** Did you bring me back any presents?

（你有買什麼禮物回來給我嗎？）

**B:** No, why would I do that?

（沒有，為什麼要買呢？）

**A:** Ah, come on, Mary, because you love me.

（少來了，瑪莉，因為你愛我啊。）

**B:** Well, I brought back some pictures you can look at.

（嗯，我帶回了一些照片給你看喔。）

**A:** Gee, thanks.

（哇，謝囉。）

**What did Mary bring back from her trip?**

（瑪莉的旅行帶回什麼東西？）

(A) Leis

(B) Pictures

(C) A coconut bra

(D) A staff

***Answer: (B)***

MP3-15（稍慢速度）
MP3-34（正常速度）

**A:** Here, John, I got you a present.

（嗨，約翰，我買了個禮物給你喔。）

**B:** What for, Mary? It's not my birthday.

（瑪莉，為什麼呢？不是我的生日啊。）

**A:** It's my way for saying I'm sorry I got mad the other day.

（我只是想用這個方式告訴你，我那天生氣真的很抱歉。）

**B:** Ah, it's all right.

（喔，沒關係啦。），

You were in a bad mood.
（你那時心情不好啊。）

**Why would Mary give John a present?**

（瑪莉為何要給約翰禮物？）

(A) To apologize

(B) Because it was her birthday

(C) Just because she was in a good mood

(D) For Christmas

***Answer: (A)***

MP3-15（稍慢速度）
MP3-34（正常速度）

**A:** Thanks, John, for watering my plants for me while I was on vacation.

（約翰，謝謝你在我度假時幫我澆花。）

**B:** It was no problem, Mary.

（瑪莉，這是件小事。）

It wasn't anything you wouldn't have done for me.
（換成是你也會幫我做的。）

**A:** That's true.

（沒錯。）

It's good to be close to your neighbors.
（和鄰居感情好真是不錯。）

**B:** That's even more true.

（這就更有道理了。）

**What did John do for Mary while Mary was on vacation?**
**（瑪莉去渡假時，約翰幫她做了什麼事？）**

(A) Pick up the mail.

(B) Get her homework for her.

(C) Take messages for her.

(D) Water her plants.

***Answer: (D)***

► Life is a sweet and joyful thing for one who has a pure conscience.

---Leo Tolstory

（心靈純淨的人，人生充滿著甜蜜和喜悅。）

-- 列夫．托爾斯泰

MP3-15（稍慢速度）
MP3-34（正常速度）

**A:** Hey, Helen, could you pick up Mary at the airport for me?

（嗨，海倫，你可以幫我去機場接瑪莉嗎？）

**B:** Why can't you do it, John?

（約翰，你自己為什麼不能去呢？）

**A:** I've got a really important meeting that just came up.

（我剛接到一個非常重要的會議。）

**B:** Yeah, I guess I could get her for you.

（好，我想我可以幫你。）

**Was John able to pick up Mary at the airport?**

（約翰可以去機場接瑪莉嗎？）

(A) Yes

(B) No

***Answer: (B)***

MP3-15（稍慢速度）
MP3-34（正常速度）

**A:** Why didn't you call me last night, John?

（約翰，你昨晚為何沒打電話給我呢？）

**B:** I was going to, but I was in a meeting and it carried over until late.

（我本來要打，但是我在開會，結束時已經很晚了。）

**A:** Well, you could have taken a break.

（那你也可以中途休息一下吧。）

**B:** No, I couldn't have called you.

（不行，我沒辦法打給你。）

The meeting was non-stop and there were no breaks.

（那個會議沒有休息時間。）

**Why didn't John call Mary?**

（約翰為何沒有打電話給瑪莉？）

(A) He forgot.

(B) He was in a meeting.

(C) He was playing a game with her.

(D) His phone broke.

***Answer: (B)***

# Dialogue

MP3-16（稍慢速度）
MP3-35（正常速度）

**A:** I haven't talked to you in a while.

（有一陣子沒跟你說話了。）

**B:** No kidding, it's been forever since last you called.

（確實是，自從上次你打給我已經不知有多久了。）

**A:** Well, you could have called me.

（嗯，你也可以打給我啊。）

So how's the weather?
（那邊天氣如何？）

**B:** Not bad. It's pretty sunny down here.

（不錯啊，天空很晴朗。）

**A:** Isn't it always that way?

（不都是這樣的嗎？）

**How is the weather?**

（天氣如何？）

(A) Sunny

(B) Rainy

(C) Snowy

(D) Cold

***Answer: (A)***

▶ Nothing great was ever achieved without enthusiasm.

---R. W. Emerrson

（沒有熱情無法成就大業。）

MP3-16（稍慢速度）
MP3-35（正常速度）

**A:** Check out these two cars.

（來看這兩部車子。）

**B:** What are they?

（是什麼車子呢？）

**A:** Come on, John.

（約翰，來吧。）

Look at them.
（你看看。）

This one is the Jaguar XJ and this one is the BMW M5.
（這部是 Jaguar XJ，另一部是 BMW M5。）

**B:** Those are some nice cars.

（都是好車呢。）

**A:** Which do you like better?

（你比較喜歡哪一部呢？）

I mean, if you could have one of them for free, which one would it be?
（我是說，如果是免費的，你會選哪一部呢？）

**B:** I think the Jaguar XJ.

（我想我會選 Jaguar XJ。）

**Which car does John like better?**
（約翰比較喜歡哪一部車？）

(A) Mazda RSX

(B) Dodge Viper

(C) Jaguar XJ

(D) BMW M5

***Answer: (C)***

MP3-16（稍慢速度）
MP3-35（正常速度）

**A:** I'm going to go to the gas station.

（我要去加油站。）

**B:** What for?

（為何？）

**A:** I need to get some cigarettes.

（我要買些香煙。）

**B:** That's a nasty habit, John.

（約翰，這不是好習慣。）

**A:** Yeah, well, I'm addicted.

（嗯，但是我已經上癮了。）

**Why is John going to the gas station?**
（約翰去加油站作什麼？）

(A) To get some gas

(B) To get some beer

(C) To get the new issue of playboy

(D) To get some cigarettes

***Answer: (D)***

MP3-16（稍慢速度）
MP3-35（正常速度）

**A:** Bob, could you give me a ride to the train station?

（鮑伯，你可以載我去火車站嗎？）

**B:** Yeah, sure. Why do you need one today, Mary?

（當然可以，瑪莉，你今天為什麼需要有人載你去？）

**A:** I forgot my umbrella.

（我忘記帶傘了。）

**B:** Ah, I see. Don't want to get a little wet, eh?

（了解，不想被雨淋濕吧？）

**Did Mary bring an umbrella with her?**

（瑪莉有隨身帶傘嗎？）

(A) Yes

(B) No

***Answer: (B)***

► Before everything else, getting ready is the secret of success.

---Henry Ford

（做好準備是成功的首要秘訣。）

MP3-16（稍慢速度）
MP3-35（正常速度）

**A:** Why would you be right for this job?

（你為什麼適合這份工作呢？）

**B:** Well, I'm honest, dependable and a hard worker.

（嗯，我很誠實，可靠，認真工作。）

**A:** Have you ever worked as a restaurant server before?

（你以前有當過餐廳服務生嗎？）

**B:** I have.

（有的。）

If you'll look at my resume right there, I put that I've worked at T. G. I. Friday and Chili's.

（你可以看看我的履歷表，上面寫著，我一直在星期五餐廳及紅番椒餐廳工作。）

**A:** Why don't you work there anymore?

（你為何不再那邊繼續工作呢？）

**B:** Location. I'd prefer working close to where I live.

（因為地點的關係，我希望能在距家近一點的地方工作。）

**What position is John applying for?**

（約翰應徵什麼工作？）

(A) Restaurant manager

(B) Restaurant server

(C) Waitress

(D) Window washer

***Answer: (B)***

# Dialogue

MP3-17（稍慢速度）
MP3-36（正常速度）

**A:** I need to go to the bank.

（我要去銀行。）

**B:** Well, you're going to have to wait.

（嗯，你還要再等等。）

It doesn't open until 10:00.
（銀行要十點才開門。）

**A:** It must be nice to be a banker.

（當個銀行人一定不錯。）

**B:** I'd love to have their hours.

（我喜歡他們的上班時間。）

**When does the bank open?**

（銀行幾點開門？）

(A) 9:00

(B) 10:00

(C) 11:00

(D) 12:00

***Answer: (B)***

▶The horizon of life is broadened chiefly by the enlargement of the heart.

---H.Blake

（生活的視野主要是隨著心胸的開闊而變得寬廣。）

----H・布萊克

# 77 Dialogue

MP3-17（稍慢速度）
MP3-36（正常速度）

**A:** I can't believe he got down on me like that.

（我真不敢相信他會這樣對待我。）

**B:** Well, what did you think he was going to do when you weren't ready for the meeting?

（嗯，你以為你沒準備好會議，他會怎麼對你呢？）

**A:** I knew he was going to chew me out but not so badly, and in front of everybody.

（我知道他會修理我，但沒想到會這麼嚴重，而且是在大家的面前。）

**B:** That'll teach you.

（讓你上了一課吧。）

## Did the meeting go well?

（會議進行的順利嗎？）

(A) Yes

(B) No

***Answer: (B)***

MP3-17（稍慢速度）
MP3-36（正常速度）

**A:** Woah, is this a new car?

（哇，這是部新車嗎？）

**B:** It sure is.

（當然囉。）

**A:** Nice, John, nice. How much was it?

（約翰，很棒，多少錢呢？）

**B:** It cost me ten grand.

（花了我一萬元。）

**A:** How much are your payments?

（你怎麼付呢？）

**B:** Three hundred a month for three years.

（每個月三百元，付三年。）

Then it's mine.
（然後車子就是我的了。）

**How much did John pay for his new car?**

（約翰付多少錢買這部車？）

(A) $5,000

(B) $10,000

(C) $15,000

(D) $20,000

***Answer: (B)***

## 79 Dialogue

MP3-17（稍慢速度）
MP3-36（正常速度）

**A:** Hey, Mary, what's for lunch?

（嗨，瑪莉，中午要吃什麼？）

**B:** I'm eating some chicken for my lunch.

（我在吃雞肉做午餐。）

I don't know what you're going to have.
（我不知道你想吃什麼。）

**A:** What? You didn't bring anything for me?

（怎不帶一些東西給我吃呢？）

**B:** And why should I?

（我為什麼要帶呢？）

**A:** Because you love me and you want me to eat well?

（因為你愛我，希望我吃的好點啊！）

**What is Mary eating?**

（瑪莉在吃什麼？）

(A) Rice

(B) Beef

(C) Chicken

(D) Peas

***Answer: (C)***

▶ Living without an aim is like sailing without a compass.

---Alexander Dumas.

（生活沒有目標，就像航海沒有指南針。）

MP3-17（稍慢速度）
MP3-36（正常速度）

**A:** Were you running?

（你剛跑步嗎？）

**B:** Yeah, how could you tell?

（是啊，你怎麼知道的？）

**A:** Well, you're all covered in sweat.

（嗯，你全身都是汗。）

Since when did you start running?
（你什麼時候開始跑步的習慣？）

**B:** I started running a couple of weeks ago.

（我幾個禮拜前開始跑步的。）

This beer belly's really gaining on me, so I needed to do something to lose weight.
（我的啤酒肚越來越大了，所以我需要想辦法減肥。）

**A:** Running definitely is a good thing to do.

（跑步確實是個不錯的運動。）

**Why is John running?**

（約翰為什麼要跑步？）

(A) For fun

(B) He's practicing for a marathon

(C) To impress a girl

(D) To lose weight

***Answer: (D)***

MP3-18（稍慢速度）
MP3-37（正常速度）

**A:** Hey John, since you got a new car, are you going to sell your old one?

（嗨，約翰，你既然有了新車，舊車是不是要賣掉呢？）

**B:** Yeah. Why? Do you need to buy a car?

（是啊，怎麼了，你需要買輛車子嗎？）

**A:** I sure do.

（沒錯。）

How much are you going to sell yours for?

（你舊車要賣多少？）

**B:** Well, I checked the blue book, and it said it's worth about five grand in its condition.

（我查過藍皮書了，書上說，以這車的現況，可以賣到五千元。）

I'd sell it to you, though, for thirty-five hundred.
（但是，我可以賣你三千五百元。）

**A:** Three thousand and you've got a deal.

（三千塊我就買了。）

**B:** Then it's a deal.

（好，那就賣你三千。）

**How much is John's used car worth?**
（約翰的舊車值多少錢？）

(A) $5,000

(B) $10,000

(C) $15,000

(D) $20,000

***Answer: (A)***

MP3-18（稍慢速度）
MP3-37（正常速度）

**A:** Who's at the door?

（門口是誰？）

**B:** It's Carol. She's here to talk to you.

（是卡羅，她來跟你説個話。）

**A:** Did you tell her I was here?

（你跟她説我在這裡嗎？）

**B:** Yes, I did. She's waiting for you.

（是的，她在等你呢。）

**A:** I told you that I didn't want to talk to her.

（我不是跟你説過我不想跟她説話。）

## Who's at the door?

（誰在門口？）

(A) Fred

(B) Allen

(C) Lisa

(D) Carol

***Answer: (D)***

▶ Do not for one repulse, give up the purpose that you resolved to effect.

---William Shakespeare

（不要只因一次失敗，就永棄你來想達到目的的決心。）

MP3-18（稍慢速度）
MP3-37（正常速度）

**A:** Can I help you find a book?

（我可以幫您找書嗎？）

**B:** Yeah, do you have To Kill a Mockingbird?

（是的，你們有「梅崗城故事」嗎？）

**A:** Yeah, let me show you where it is.

（是的，我跟您説擺在哪裡。）

**B:** Thanks, I've been looking for it for a while.

（謝謝你，我找了好久了。）

**A:** Oh, it's no problem.

（噢，別客氣。）

**Which book was the man looking for?**

（這男人在找什麼書？）

(A) To Kill a Mockingbird

(B) Grapes of Wrath

(C) War and Peace

(D) The Rats of Nimh

***Answer: (A)***

►A man can succeed at almost anything for which he has unlimited enthusiasm. ----Charles Schwab

---Pasteur

（一個人，只要他有無限的熱情，就幾乎可以在任何事情上取得成功。）

MP3-18（稍慢速度）
MP3-37（正常速度）

**A:** Do you have the book, Man in the High Castle?

（你們有沒有「高塔裡的男人」這本書？）

**B:** Hmm, never heard of it. Who's it by?

（嗯，沒聽過，是誰寫的？）

**A:** Philip K. Dick.

（飛利浦 ・ 迪克。）

**B:** Never heard of him, either.

（也沒聽過這個作者。）

Let me check the computer.
（我來查查電腦。）

**A:** Would you? Thanks.

（那就謝謝你了。）

**B:** No, it's not showing up on the computer. Sorry.

（還是沒有，電腦也查不到，抱歉。）

**Does the bookstore carry the book the man is looking for?**
（這家書店有這男人要找的書嗎？）

(A) Yes

(B) No

***Answer: (B)***

MP3-18（稍慢速度）
MP3-37（正常速度）

**A:** Who are you on the phone with?

（你在跟誰講電話？）

**B:** Nobody.

（沒有人啊。）

**A:** Come on, Mary, you don't normally talk on the phone to nobody.

（少來了，瑪莉，正常人不會拿著無人的電話講話。）

Who are you talking to?
（你到底在跟誰講電話啊？）

**B:** Jack.

（傑克。）

**A:** And what does he want?

（他要做什麼？）

**B:** He wants to come over and watch a movie.

（他想過來看部電影。）

Is that all right?

（可以嗎？）

**With whom is Mary talking on the phone?**

（瑪莉跟誰在講電話呢？）

(A) John

(B) Caroline

(C) Jack

(D) Bob

***Answer: (C)***

MP3-19（稍慢速度）
MP3-38（正常速度）

**A:** I'm home!

（我回家了！）

**B:** So I see.

（我看到啦。）

**A:** What? You're not glad to see me?

（怎麼了，你看到我不開心嗎？）

You're not going to welcome me with a kiss?
（你不親我一下來歡迎我嗎？）

**B:** Hmm now that you mention it, no.

（嗯，既然你提了，答案是否定的。）

Did you pick up anything for us to eat?
（你有沒有買什麼回來吃呢？）

**A:** Is that all I am to you?

（對你來說，我就是這樣嗎？）

Make money and buy you food.
（賺錢然後買東西給你吃。）

**What did the man first say when he got home?**
（這男人一到家先說了什麼？）

(A) Hey Mary, where are you?

(B) Hey, how are you doing?

(C) I'm back!

(D) I'm home!

***Answer: (D)***

# 87 Dialogue

MP3-19（稍慢速度）
MP3-38（正常速度）

**A:** Where are you going?

（你要去哪裡？）

**B:** To my favorite place on Earth.

（去我最想去的地方。）

**A:** Where is that?

（那是哪裡呢？）

**B:** Cici's Pizza. Where else?

（西西披薩，除了那裡還會有哪裡？）

**A:** A pizza place?

（披薩店？）

**B:** You don't understand.

（你不了解的。）

That place is awesome.

（那個地方很棒。）

The pizza is the best I’ve ever had.
（他們的披薩是我吃過最好吃的。）

**Where is the women's favorite place?**
（這個人最喜歡的地方是哪裡？）

(A) The park

(B) His parents’ house

(C) The lake

(D) Cici's Pizza

***Answer: (D)***

MP3-19（稍慢速度）
MP3-38（正常速度）

**A:** So you didn't bring me anything to eat, huh?

（你沒買東西給我吃？）

**B:** Nope, I didn't.

（沒，我沒買。）

**A:** Well, do you want to go out to eat?

（嗯，那你想出去吃嗎？）

**B:** I guess we could.

（我想可以吧。）

**A:** How about Mack's Diner?

（去麥克餐廳吃好嗎？）

**B:** Sounds good to me.

（我覺得不錯啊。）

**Where are they going for dinner?**

（他們要去哪裡吃晚餐？）

(A) Mack's Diner

(B) Covino's Pizza

(C) Pizza Hut

(D) Frank's Burgers

***Answer: (A)***

MP3-19（稍慢速度）
MP3-38（正常速度）

**A:** Are you going tonight?

（你今晚要去嗎？）

**B:** Going to what?

（去哪裡？）

**A:** The opening of the new building at the university.

（學校新大樓的啟用儀式。）

**B:** Why would I go?

（為什麼要去呢？）

**A:** The mayor's going to be there.

（市長會去。）

**B:** So?

（那又怎樣？）

**A:** There'll be free food.

（還會有免費的食物。）

**B:** Oh, well then, I'm there.

（噢，那我會去。）

**What event is it?**

（是什麼事件？）

(A) The opening night of a theater production.

(B) The opening of a new building at the university.

(C) The opening night of a new movie.

(D) The Cowboys – Texans game.

***Answer: (B)***

MP3-19（稍慢速度）
MP3-38（正常速度）

**A:** Did you see Mary's new puppy?

（你有看到瑪莉新買的小狗嗎？）

**B:** Oh, it's adorable, isn't it?

（喔，很可愛啊，不是嗎？）

**A:** I wish Jack would let us get a puppy.

（我希望傑克願意讓我們養隻小狗。）

**B:** What, he doesn't like dogs?

（什麼，他不喜歡狗？）

**A:** Not at all. What about Joe?

（他一點也不喜歡，喬喜歡嗎？）

**B:** No, he doesn't, either.

（不，他也不喜歡狗。）

**What are the two women talking about?**
（這兩 個女人在討論什麼？）

(A) Mary's new puppy

(B) Mary's and John's fight

(C) The opening of the new building at the university.

(D) The new restaurant on the corner.

***Answer: (A)***

MP3-20（稍慢速度）
MP3-39（正常速度）

**A:** Hey, John. What have you been up to?

（嗨，約翰，最近都在忙什麼啊？）

**B:** I've been practicing a lot with the school team.

（我最近都在校隊練習。）

**A:** Oh, what do you play?

（你是在什麼校隊？）

**B:** Soccer.

（足球。）

**What kind of school team is John in?**

（約翰在什麼校隊？）

(A) Math

(B) Football

(C) Soccer

(D) Chess

***Answer: (C)***

▶ Nothing great was ever achieved without enthusiasm.

---R.W.Emerson

（沒有熱情無法成就大業。）

--R・W・愛默生

MP3-20（稍慢速度）
MP3-39（正常速度）

**A:** Hey John, I heard you got a new car.

（嗨，約翰，我聽説你買了輛新車。）

**B:** Yeah, I did.

（是啊，我是買了車。）

**A:** Is it pretty nice?

（車子還好嗎？）

**B:** It's awesome. I love it.

（棒極了，我愛死了。）

**A:** What kind is it?

（是哪型的車呢？）

**B:** It's a Toyota Camry.

（是豐田的 Camry。）

**What did John get?**

（約翰買了新的什麼？）

(A) A new puppy

(B) A new set of golf clubs

(C) A new car

(D) A new cat

***Answer: (C)***

▶I succeeded because I willed it; I never hesitated.

----Napolen

（我成功是因為我有決心，從不猶豫。）

MP3-20（稍慢速度）
MP3-39（正常速度）

**A:** What did you get for Christmas, Mary?

（瑪莉，你聖誕禮物拿到什麼？）

**B:** I got a new piano.

（我得到一台新鋼琴。）

**A:** Woah, that's a big Christmas present.

（哇，這可是份很大的聖誕禮物呢。）

**B:** Yeah, it is.

（是啊。）

I've been begging for one for years.
（我已經求了很多年。）

I mean, what's the point of taking lessons if you don't have a piano?
（我是說，如果沒有鋼琴，去上課又有什麼用呢？）

**A:** No kidding.

（沒錯。）

**Did Mary get the piano for her birthday present?**

（瑪莉得到鋼琴作為生日禮物嗎？）

(A) Yes, she got the piano for her birthday.

(B) No, she got the piano for Christmas.

(C) No, she bought the piano herself.

(D) No, she got the piano for Easter.

***Answer: (B)***

▶Before everything else, getting ready is the secret of success.

---Henry Ford

（做好準備是成功的首要秘訣。）

- 亨利 · 福特

MP3-20（稍慢速度）
MP3-39（正常速度）

**A:** I heard there was some pretty bad weather down there.

（我聽說你那邊的天氣很糟。）

**B:** Yeah, John, those hurricanes got pretty bad.

（是啊，約翰，龍捲風颳得很嚴重。）

How's the weather over there?
（你那邊天氣如何？）

**A:** Not bad. Just a light rain.

（還不錯，只有下點小雨。）

We've needed it.
（我們正需要雨。）

It's been pretty hot and dry lately.
（最近天氣都太熱又太乾燥了。）

**B:** Well, we've had enough rain.

（嗯，我們的雨已經很夠了。）

**How's the weather where John's at?**
（約翰那邊的天氣如何？）

(A) Sunny

(B) Hurricanes

(C) A light rain

(D) Hot and dry

***Answer: (C)***

▶Resolve to perform what you ought; perform without fail what you resolve.

---Benjamin Franklin

（應該做的決心去做，決心做的就務必去做。）

MP3-20（稍慢速度）
MP3-39（正常速度）

**A:** What are you doing with the printer?

（你為什麼在弄印表機啊？）

**B:** I'm trying to fix it.

（我在試著修理它啊。）

**A:** What happened to it?

（它怎麼了？）

**B:** A paper jam.

（夾紙。）

Darned thing keeps jamming up.
（這可惡的東西一直在卡紙。）

## What happened to the printer?

（這台印表機怎麼了？）

(A) It was stolen.

(B) It disappeared.

(C) Johnny took it home with him.

(D) The paper keeps jamming.

***Answer: (D)***

▶Do not, for one repulse, give up the purpose that you resolved to effect.

----William Shakespeare

（不要只因一次失敗，就放棄你原來想達到目的的決心。）

# 聽霸 英語聽力模擬測驗

英語系列：48

作者／張瑪麗 Steve King
出版者／哈福企業有限公司
地址／新北市板橋區五權街16號
電話／(02) 2945-6285　傳真／(02) 2945-6986
郵政劃撥／31598840　戶名／哈福企業有限公司
出版日期／2018年5月
定價／NT$ 329元 (附MP3)

全球華文國際市場總代理／采舍國際有限公司
地址／新北市中和區中山路2段366巷10號3樓
電話／(02) 8245-8786　傳真／(02) 8245-8718
網址／www.silkbook.com 新絲路華文網

香港澳門總經銷／和平圖書有限公司
地址／香港柴灣嘉業街12號百樂門大廈17樓
電話／(852) 2804-6687　傳真／(852) 2804-6409
定價／港幣110元 (附MP3)

圖片／shuttlestock
email／haanet68@Gmail.com
網址／Haa-net.com
facebook／Haa-net 哈福網路商城



國家圖書館出版品預行編目資料

聽霸 英語聽力模擬測驗 / 張瑪麗, Steve King著. -- 新北市：哈福企業, 2018.05
面；　公分. -- (英語系列；48)

ISBN 978-986-96282-0-4(平裝附光碟片)

1. 多益測驗

805.1895　　107007196

哈福

哈福

哈福